# CRITICAL
## TIM

**Also by Tim Sebastian**

*The Spy In Question*
*Spy Shadow*
*Saviour's Gate*

## About the Author

**Tim Sebastian** was born in London in 1952. For over ten years he reported for the BBC, mainly from Eastern Europe. As the BBC's correspondent in Warsaw, he witnessed the rise of Solidarity and went on to cover the complete disintegration of the Soviet Bloc. He was the BBC's first television correspondent in Moscow, but was expelled in 1985 for 'activities not compatible with his status'. The Soviet security services later described him as a British Intelligence operative who worked for the BBC under the code name 'Timosha'. Tim Sebastian denied these charges. He now lives in London, where he divides his time between writing and broadcasting.

# EXIT BERLIN

# TIM SEBASTIAN

**BANTAM BOOKS**
TORONTO • NEW YORK • LONDON • SYDNEY • AUCKLAND

EXIT BERLIN

A BANTAM BOOK 0 553 40258 7

Originally published in Great Britain by Bantam Press, a division of Transworld Publishers Ltd.

PRINTING HISTORY
Bantam Press edition published 1992
Bantam Books edition published 1993

Set in 10½/13½pt Melior by
County Typesetters, Margate, Kent

Bantam Books are published by Transworld Publishers Ltd, 61–63 Uxbridge Road, Ealing, London W5 5SA, in Australia by Transworld Publishers (Australia) Pty Ltd, 15–23 Helles Avenue, Moorebank, NSW 2170, and in New Zealand by Transworld Publishers (NZ) Ltd, 3 William Pickering Drive, Albany, Auckland.

Made and printed in Great Britain by
Cox & Wyman Ltd, Reading, Berks.

For Joni and Sylva

# PROLOGUE

When I watch her – when I watch her lips open into a promise, and her eyes soften with tears – then my doubts go away. I know where she comes from and where she's going.

Sometimes she gets up well before dawn, believing I'm still asleep. She sits by the window, staring at the city, searching maybe for a shadow or a face from the past.

I never ask her about those times and she never tells me. But we all need a secret place to go to – especially the people who say they don't. And in this business there are always things we don't want to tell ourselves and questions we don't want to ask. So let her have her peace and her thoughts. I don't want to own her.

Unlike me she hasn't aged with the passing of the years. For as the poets tell us – some qualities are eternal and she has more than her share. She's just as kind and as caring as ever. And there's still the same quicksilver mind that wants to see good, where I would see evil.

Our passion, too, has survived the years, if

anything it is more intense, and more satisfying than in the early days of the relationship. By the standards of all that is valuable I have much to be thankful for.

So why do my doubts return?

Maybe it's the missing pieces in both our lives – the long absences, the unaccounted contacts.

I still think of the years in what was then East Germany – when I was forced to live without her. But I'm no longer angry. I no longer see the time as wasted. She has taught me to draw benefit from my experiences – even those that seemed dark and empty.

But could she have saved me earlier? Could she have fought to clear my name in the days when it was spoken with only hatred and contempt? Even after all this time I don't know if she stays with me out of pity. I don't know whether it was she who betrayed me.

I only know I can never bring myself to ask her.

# ONE

I knew it was going to end.

That rainy night in October, and I was slinking home late along the side-streets and alleys of the Normannenstrasse, when the good citizens of East Berlin were in bed, and the bad ones were working over there – in that city within a city, the compound, the headquarters of the East German Security Service – as it was then.

The lights were on in the 26th Abteilung. Counter-intelligence, surveillance – all on overtime in those days of protest and pressure.

The rain began to fling itself hard against the houses and the wind picked up and I stepped into a doorway and shook myself like a rat.

And then I saw it – the tiny, quiet convoy – two trucks, an armoured car in front, three black Volgas behind, the little troupe that had no markings of any kind – but to me, just to me, had 'Soviet' written all over it.

You could barely hear the engines, just the swish of tyres on the wet cobbles.

The vehicles turned and stopped before the main

gate, and one man emerged from a Volga, looked round sharply and tapped on the roof.

And I forgot about the rain and the discomfort and the cold that seeped steadily under my skin. Such a dark night, that one, but not dark enough to obscure what happened.

They were running then for the doors and I could see the little latch-gate open and the guard from the dawn shift peering through and suddenly the whole area seemed full of troops with sub-machine-guns and men in dark raincoats, only no shouts or orders.

They must have fired with a silencer because I saw the guard go down fast, and another – and not a sound as the rain drummed down beside me.

They hurried inside, leaving two guards on the gate in the uniforms of East Germany's army.

Maybe I'm only guessing at what happened next, the sprint down the corridors, a few Stasi people dying where they stood, a scream, a look of horror and no time for anything else.

I stood with my heart counting out the seconds double time, and it can't have been long before the first of the trucks was backing to the main gate and the big grey boxes were being loaded from trolleys.

They were taking the files, I told myself, barely able to form the words. The crown jewels of the East German State. Lifting their security files in the middle of East Berlin . . .

I must have held my breath, lest they hear me or see the vapour in that winter morning.

Three, four, five minutes . . . what does it matter? But the first truck must have been full, for the second was already pulling forward to take its place, the tailgate open and more men inside to shovel the filing cases.

Who do you tell, Martin, I thought? Murder and treason on the grandest of scales. And you don't tell anyone, do you? You watch and you wait, and you see where it leads.

The dawn shift on. Perfect time to do it. In those days each section was shortstaffed – all their considerable resources being used to quell the demonstrations and pacify the ringleaders. Jails were full, interrogations going on round the clock. Counter-propaganda. Only East Germany would have read the writing on the wall and tried to erase it.

They were shutting the tailgate now. They must have been very selective, knew what they were going for, had it all worked out to the last detail, with their own people on the inside, and maps and all that sort of thing . . .

Engines running again and they're back in formation, moving the way they'd come. They'd be in a hurry now. Sure they would. They'd head for the airport at Schönefeld, military section, cargo plane, emergency transport, out of our way comrades, the Soviet Union is on the move. I could hear it all, because if you've ever lived in East Berlin, you know how the Russians do it – chucking their weight around, the older, stronger cousin, taking the best of everything. Just the way they'd done it before my eyes.

Sirens now, getting closer. Probably Stasi troops, from the two divisions they were never supposed to have inside the city. Picture it, Martin. They've been so badly stung that when they search the streets you don't want to be on them. All those unlisted phones ringing madly across the city, and all those oh-so-photographed faces rising from pillows to curse the day they'd been born.

The rain helped me hurry, drenching me the moment I stepped from the doorway. Then I ran for it, taking the side-streets, scuffing my shoes, catching my raincoat, and in the end I couldn't hear the sirens any longer and I walked the rest of the way home.

East Berlin really did look as lousy as it was cracked up to be. Half the streetlamps weren't working, tramlines criss-crossed the cobbles, piles of rubble lay all about me.

But what, I wondered, do you care about any of it?

I stood still inside the main door of the apartment block to make sure no one was awake, and then I took the stone stairs and let myself in. No lights. I went straight to the bedroom, removed my wet clothes and put on a dressing-gown.

In the kitchen I spilled coffee on my hand and stubbed my toe on the table and at least that provided some minor distraction. For, as I sat at the table, it occurred to me that the Russians had simply gone in and removed the most valuable files from the East German collection. Why? Because they believed the regime was about to be toppled. That Communism here was dying and that very little time remained.

So, when I finally pulled the sheets over my head, and the rough cheap blanket they'd given me when I'd first arrived – I knew it was finished.

Why am I not surprised that they didn't mention any of this on the morning news programme, neither on radio, nor television, nor on any of the Western stations, blaring out to us from the other side of the Wall? Weren't they supposed to be so well informed?

At work too – in my section, in all the other offices, in the canteen gossip and the little shop, so well-stocked with all the privileged goods, that all the ordinary mortals could only dream about ... silence. Complete and utter silence. No added tension, no departmental witch-hunts. No extra-solemn faces, although how could you tell?

So, I waited a day and then sent a message, by the only route they'd ever told me to use, the keep-it-for-Armageddon route, the once-only route, the last-best-moment route.

I'm alive, I told them, but the place is disintegrating. I have to get out. I'm coming home and I'm bringing my basket of treasures with me.

I sent it all right, but there was no reply.

# TWO

I was the only one left in East Berlin on the day the Wall came down.

Most people went over on foot, even from my block. I saw them, scuttling down the street, well before dawn, carrier bags in hand, glancing occasionally over their shoulder just to make sure no one had noticed.

There were the Glicks with their two boys, noses dripping like faulty taps; Frau Ansbach, fat and fruity, always an eye open for things in trousers; and Dortmunder the dark, soulful student who, everyone said, was a poet.

At about nine o'clock he knocked on my door and stammered . . . 'Herr Martin, aren't you go . . .' but then he stopped himself, because, like all the others, he knew, didn't he? I'd never told any of them but they knew just the same. This wasn't East Berlin for nothing.

I can't forget that day, handed down as it was, like a death sentence.

It was past two before I ventured out, and the

November leaves were gusting across the cobble-stones. Above me the clouds raced westwards, the way everyone else had gone. Like a city struck by an earthquake, East Berlin had been abandoned where it lay, its walls and citadels, guarding only the dead and the fearful.

Among whose numbers I counted myself.

I could have gone to the checkpoint, but there wasn't much point. One look at my documents and the border police would have found me a special little room with a special little person to talk to – because, after all, there were some things that didn't close down that day. I know that now.

Walking north from my place, I crossed the Schönhauser Allee and came to the back streets that are largely untamed and untouched since the Nazis died in them. Proud houses, they must have been. Now blackened and scarred, the bullets, half a century old, embedded in the plaster.

I had wondered if I'd see him that day – the old soldier who seemed to live in the little park across from the *Gasthaus*. He of the old brown jacket and dusty trousers, the face a mass of beard and whiskers like an overgrown garden. He had been in that same park on the day the Red Army had subdued it – along with a few mothers, and cats and children. And he had watched them die, hoping they'd have the grace to finish him off as well. But they hadn't, choosing instead to leave him alive so that he could tell the world – and go mad in the process.

He had fulfilled both expectations, just as they'd known he would.

But he wasn't there on that November day to ease the awful peace and stillness.

My mother used to say loneliness was a gift. She had come from a family of five children, so I could see what she meant. But I'd never shared the feeling. Not then. Not now either.

And she hadn't mentioned it that time in '86 when she came to visit, finding out, she said, how 'a son of hers could do a thing like that'.

As I sat in the park, I could recall the little figure so clearly, scared out of her wits, frail and delicate as a spring breeze, crossing Checkpoint Charlie, blue Burberry belted tightly around her, British passport clasped in front of her to ward off evil.

She had seen me when she was still some way from the final exit, a scattering of day-trippers ahead of her, and I could almost feel her heart heave. The twin emotions of love and disappointment tearing it in two.

Through the barrier then and she seemed to hug me and push me away at the same time.

In a dismal café on the Alexanderplatz we waited forty minutes for coffee, lukewarm and grainy. She hadn't eaten that day but she wouldn't eat with me.

'How could you ... ?' she kept asking. And I couldn't find the words, staring through the net

17

curtains as the rain bucketed down on to the square.

She made me remember all the things I had tried so hard to forget. Little things, British things, the tiny details that make up the grand design. Picnics, birthday parties, the successes and failures of childhood. Friends who'd 'asked about you', times with Dad and the cousins, the seaside, fish and chips.

'Everyone was so very upset,' she whispered. In fact she whispered the whole time she was in East Berlin. And I couldn't blame her for that. After all the Stasi had set up whole factories to produce their bugging equipment. That was the comforting thing about this place. However bad you thought it was, you were probably right.

When the cloudburst was over I walked her back to the checkpoint. She looked even paler than before. Her eyes so bright and heavy from all the tears. And I remembered standing in the kitchen such a long time ago. 'Don't cry Mum,' I heard the little voice saying. But now I couldn't say it any more.

Just before the barrier, she turned and held me tightly, the way she always used to. For my mum there were never any half measures. She would love with passion and hate with passion. Nothing in the middle.

'You're still my son, and I'll always love you,' she whispered. 'But I can't forgive what you did.'

She turned away, and I'll never know why it was that I couldn't move – because I wanted to run after her, the way a child follows its mother. Only this time I really couldn't, watching her till she was out of sight, the blue raincoat disappearing among all the uniforms and tourists. She was probably on a plane and halfway back to England by the time I left the checkpoint and went home.

Nearly three years have passed since my mother died without ever seeing me again – her son, the traitor, assembling all his memories on that grey November afternoon, as the wall around East Berlin tumbled into history, and the rain began again.

I should have expected it. But the years of intrigue and deception have left me strangely naïve – over-anxious to trust people, daring myself to take risks, taunting the devil.

And you can do that only for so long.

He was sitting by the living-room fire when I got back from the park. In the semi-darkness his shadow made him seem larger than he probably was.

I was aware of a bulky coat and a felt hat. A small puddle had formed around the hearth as the rain dripped off him. He can't have been there long.

'Herr Martin?'

'What do you want?'

And that seemed to pass for our greeting.

He was by no means the first of the unannounced visitors. Over the years there had been quite a selection – the cocky ones who'd made themselves coffee and leafed through my books, the aggressive kind who'd flung me around the room a bit just to drive home their point, the weak and helpless – who had turned out not to be.

But on that day of all days, I had thought to have seen the last of them.

I must have gasped in surprise for the figure shifted uncomfortably in his seat. The voice was gruff and uneducated. 'There is no reason to be alarmed Herr Martin.' And why, I wondered, did I always doubt assurances of that kind most of all?

I sat down across the coffee table.

'The events of the last few hours . . .'

'It's happened so suddenly,' I prompted.

He nodded his head vigorously. 'For us, Herr Martin, not quite so sudden. Shall we say that the wind had been blowing in that direction for several months.' He smiled, apparently pleased with the metaphor. I caught sight of a line of teeth, with plenty of gaps.

'Of course there are changes.' He waved a hand towards the street. 'And I think to myself . . . who would be a good person in Berlin to discuss these changes? Who would understand the West, who would understand the new order, and the ways to survive and prosper? And then I remember . . .

Herr Martin.' The voice trailed away. Outside, a car engine was switched off. But there was no opening of doors, no sound of boots on the cobbles. I put it out of my mind.

'I understand what you're saying.'

'I think not, Herr Martin. Let me be clearer. I have held a post in State Security for many years. I learned many interesting things. I learned about many interesting people.' He paused. 'I learned quite a few things about you . . .'

And it was only then that an old, rough hand seemed to shake me awake. I was suddenly acutely aware of everything in the room. I slowed my breathing. I concentrated on making no move of any kind, no flutter of the eyelids. All I needed to do was listen.

'Herr Martin, because of my dealings with the other socialist states, including the Soviet Union, I acquired sensitive and sometimes vital information. Names and information. To be frank with you, I would now be in a position to trade such information in return for certain favours from the new authorities.'

He looked at me as if waiting for approval.

'I cannot advise you on this,' I cleared my throat.

'And if I were to tell you I had information about a traitor in the British Service . . . ?' He raised his eyebrows. 'What would you tell me then, Herr Martin?'

I looked at him blankly – and that was no act. He

could have been setting one of a dozen traps. And yet why should he bother now? Didn't his story hold up? Wouldn't Eastern Europe be crawling with Stasi, falling over themselves to sell their stories, in return for money or position, or immunity from the law?

'Think about this for twenty-four hours, Herr Martin. We will talk again.'

In that moment, of course, I should have stopped him leaving, forced him to tell me what was going on, who he was. And yet I'd been so long in the East that I took his visit as normal. Any thug with an identity card could barge into your home, dictate his terms and rip your life apart in the name of the People – there were generations growing up here, knowing nothing else.

And I think I became aware in that moment, as he carefully buttoned his coat that this whole business wasn't really over. If he had sought to bring me any message at all, even in his cryptic, bullying way – it was that.

I listened to his footsteps on the staircase, then turned to the window. For some reason I wanted to watch the way he walked. Did he still have the Stasi's swagger and bravado, was he still part of the élite, or would he slink off into the urban undergrowth like a beaten animal?

When he hit the street he was in a hurry. His head turned left and right, and then there was a small wave – as if he had recognized someone. He hurried across the street, and I could see a black Volga with shaded windows about thirty yards from him under the trees. He broke into a run, and then he must have missed his footing for he keeled over hard on to his side. And it struck me as odd even then for he didn't put out his hands to break the fall, and he wasn't moving on the ground, wasn't rising to his feet. From the corner of my eye I could see the Volga tear away from the kerb, its tyres snatching at the cobbles . . . and then it hit me why no one had come out to help him, and by now the Volga was halfway down the street, its brake lights flashing briefly at the intersection.

I ran to the door and took the steps three at a time, and still there was nothing and no one on the streets.

He lay face down, his hat a few feet away, and as I bent low I could see the fresh blood already drying on his cheek. The bullet, I realized, must have entered just above the bridge of the nose. And it wasn't until the thought had struck me that I turned away in revulsion, taking off my jacket, strewing it haphazardly over the coated shape in the road, standing shivering and quite alone in the silence of East Berlin – where that day, of all days, you could die so suddenly and without a prayer.

I don't know where they came from – the militia. I don't know who called them. I didn't really know they still existed – that night when the border came down.

But after a minute, two at most, I could see the flashing lights a long way down the street, long before I could hear the sirens. Three cars, nine officers, a couple of extras in suits and ties to do the reading and writing.

I just stood where I was, as they examined the body, then deposited it, still in my jacket, in the back of their van.

A grey suit approached me. 'Looks like a heart attack,' he said.

I didn't argue. Looking back, I can't see what it would have achieved.

They were still playing mirrors and shadows, and for the little time left to them, day would be night and night would be day – just as it always had been. Their definitions were the only ones that ever counted.

I went upstairs, and I remember bitterly regretting my lost jacket. At about ten I heard the Glicks return, the boys yelling and scrapping on the staircase. Then a giggle and a low muttering – clear evidence that Frau Ansbach had got lucky on some outing and brought her souvenir home.

In my kitchen, as the hours melted past me, and the coffee flooded through me, and my teeth chattered in the draught from the window, it seemed almost a night like any other – unless you counted everything else.

# THREE

I had always dreaded the dawn over East Berlin. At least when it was dark you could cherish the illusion that you were somewhere else. Daylight, though, brought fresh disappointment to the shoddy, winding streets along the Schönhauser Allee.

In the distance, over breakfast, there was for ever the television tower – no thing of beauty. It was, they said, one of the highest of its kind and a magnificent achievement. Here, of course, they were always achieving. Nothing ever got done – but by God they achieved. Results, medals, progress – even a wall, the anti-fascist protection barrier, they called it and if that came down, they always said, it could lead to war.

The day was Tuesday. Tense, cold. The radio said they were streaming over in their thousands into the West. The heating had broken down in my flat. But no war.

I put my coat on over my pyjamas and shuffled to the kiosk on the corner, unshaven, an English cap on my head. I bought a comb and a packet of envelopes because that's all they had – and I wasn't going to come back with nothing. But of course there were no newspapers and the woman at the kiosk didn't mention a body on the street, with a felt hat close to it, and a borrowed tweed jacket used as a shroud.

And try as I might I couldn't feel much remorse for my visitor – the little opportunist, seeking to buy himself a fine slice of the new life by trading a filthy slice of the old.

His own people would have got to him, or maybe another of the East Europeans. If he'd had that many secrets in his head, it was miraculous that he'd lasted as long as he had. But then if he'd passed those secrets to me . . .

It wasn't a line of thought I felt like continuing. I'd already decided to get out, but now it was quite possible I was being watched. If I made any kind of hurried move they'd cut me down, same as the visitor.

I tried to shake the confusion from my mind. It was a long time since I'd dealt with such a tangible threat.

As I reached the third floor I could see Frau Ansbach standing in my doorway, right hand on hip, right hip encased in straining black leather. On her sweater writhed a grotesque python-like brooch. She pushed out her breasts towards me – truly the last things I wanted that morning.

'So, Herr Martin . . . So, I have been over there to do some shopping, *na ja*.'

She had already opened the door, so I gestured for her to come inside. Evidently she wanted congratulations.

'I'm delighted Frau Ansbach . . .'

'*Ist gut – na*? We sat in a café until till two in the morning and had some drinks. Super. Really super.'

I had visions of a can of coke being passed round with six straws.

'But that is wonderful, Frau Ansbach.'

'Monika, Herr Martin. You must call me Monika, no?'

'Of course Monika . . .'

'And I shall call you James. *Richtig ja*?'

She eyed me cautiously. Perhaps it was all rather sudden. And yet her trip to the West had given her something the Communist State had never managed. Equality. She was now my equal, and wanted me to know it.

She sat at the kitchen table and leafed through magazines – an old *Newsweek*, a couple of journals from Moscow. She would take her time and then, I felt sure, she would mention the body. Not even a rat could sneeze on that street without her hearing. She had to know.

'Herr Martin . . . I mean James . . .'

'Yes, Monika.'

'We were wondering, Frau Glick and myself, not of course that we normally discuss such things . . .' she stopped and looked at the floorboards. In the light you could see she was heavily made up, enough foundation to start a decent block of flats, lipstick teasingly applied. 'We were wondering how it was you came to leave your country for . . .' her hand described a vague circle, 'for all this. I mean the shops and things over there . . .' The voice died away into a self-conscious mumble.

We didn't look at each other and I hid my confusion.

Four years I had known her and she had never even dared to ask what country I came from. Four years during which she had ogled me from her upstairs window with the unspoken promise of her creaky old bed. Four years during which I lay awake under her room hearing that bed employed in all manner of extravagant functions. Four years of winks and nods, and 'It's better not to ask' shrugs. And she had chosen this day to ask why I'd come over. What's more she didn't know.

'We all have our reasons . . .' I looked at her warily.

She toyed with a teaspoon.

'I suppose you will be going home, *nicht wahr*? Everyone, they say, is free to go or come.'

'I haven't thought about it,' I lied.

'Of course not. *This* is your home. Not too bad uh?' She licked her bright red lipstick. 'So,' she said softly and got up. And it was at that moment that I almost felt sorry for her. I caught sight of her laddered tights and the scuffed high heels. You're a shabby old tart, I thought. But I did feel sorry for her, without knowing the reason why.

And then quite suddenly she sat down again, businesslike, engaged, her mind made up – about something.

'I should speak to you.' Pause. 'James.'

'We were speaking, Monika.' I could feel myself trying to smile encouragingly.

And then I saw it, the tear, large and glistening in her right eye, and all the more remarkable to be spawned from this brash, over-sexed East Berliner, who, surely, would never have entertained a thought worth crying over.

I made coffee while she summoned her thoughts from whatever tiny, out of the way drawer in which she kept them.

She sipped from the cup and then put it down. 'So, I say this now and then we forget about it, OK?'

'Whatever you want, Monika.'

She wouldn't look at me. Her eyes ranged around the kitchen, glancing at everything else – but not me.

'You remember when you came here? *Ja*?'

'*Ja*.'

'They called round – of course, you know who I mean . . .'

I nodded.

'Said to me, "Herr Martin is from the West, nice man, important man, very clever." They said you were special, Herr Martin, James.' She looked at me for the first time. 'But like clever man, you were forgetful, eccentric. I was to watch you, make sure you were all right.' She wiped away the tear. It was a practised gesture. I'd been wrong. This one had cried before.

'First it was every month.' Frau Ansbach shut her eyes. 'I would go to this building – their city – the Normannenstrasse. Took twenty minutes on the U-Bahn. They never even offered to pay.' She pouted. 'And then the questions . . . what you did, what time you came home, the people you went with . . . that blonde thing who used to visit.' She blushed. 'I don't know what she . . . Anyway that wasn't enough. They called me again and again . . .'

'But we hardly ever spoke.'

'I made it up.'

'You what?' And at that moment I couldn't help laughing at her – the old crone, squeezed into her leather skirt, looking like a sack tied up in the middle. I shook my head, 'Really Monika, you had a nerve. What did you tell them?'

'That you were good in bed, that you drank too much, ate too much and often slandered the State . . .'

'And they believed you?'

'They were pleased. Once they even gave me money – five thousand marks in small notes.' She grinned. 'Just like thieves.'

I leaned back on my chair and studied her, but she had clearly had enough.

'I have wanted to tell you this for a long time. Now it's better.'

We both stood up and for some unaccountable reason shook hands, as if an old debt had finally been settled.

Only it struck me, as she swung those ample hips through my doorway, that nothing had been settled at all. Maybe she had been testing me. Maybe she was watching me more closely than she'd ever admitted.

Frau Ansbach, they all said, the Stasi whore, loved the uniform, loved the perks, loved it, upwards, downwards, hanging from the ceiling, any way they wanted it.

Get out tonight, I told myself. Once they're all in bed, screwing and spying on each other and playing God knows what kind of convoluted game. Get out before they have you bleeding into some East Berlin gutter and the world moves away without you.

I went for lunch at the *Gasthaus* on the corner of the Pankower Strasse. A whole group were whingeing and dribbling into their goulash soup. Every second word was *Mauer* – wall. Wall this, wall that. I sat at a table by myself and felt like screaming.

Dortmunder was in the middle of them. I could feel him pointing me out to the others. That's Herr Martin – the Englishman, he would tell them. Nobody really knows what he's doing here. And then the wink, because of course they did. 'He'll be well up shit creek now,' someone snorted. They looked round to see if I'd heard.

I watched them wolf their food, spitting it all over the table-cloth in their excitement. Like animals, they were, raised in captivity, then shown the gate of the zoo and told they could walk through it. So what did they do? Took a few steps the first day, a few more the second, by the end of the week they'd gone deep into the jungle and acted as if they owned it. Another month, and they would say it all stank anyway, and go back to their cages, or would they?

I knew a lot about cages. Like the first few months in East Berlin and Moscow, all those years ago, when it was really seductive to live in the zoo. Meals found, flat found, money found, no need to make choices because they either made them for you, or there weren't any.

That was the first turn when you came over the Wall. And then you waited and dreaded the second. Much more painful, much harder to manage. The first cold droplet of doubt, the shifting values, the avalanche of regret. Whatever way you came across the Wall, whatever your motive, there was no escaping the second turn.

I ordered chicken. '*Einmal Broiler*,' I told Herr Winkler. He sniffed and shook his head.

'No Broiler. Have the goulash. It's better.'

'It wasn't yesterday.'

Colour flooded into his fat cheeks. 'Then go over the Wall, Herr Martin, and eat the shitty food they have there.' He slammed a plate on the counter.

I could have punched him then. I could have leaned over and seized his outsize nose and slammed his head back against the bar-room mirror. Over the years I had wanted to do that so often – to all of them. Instead I told him, 'Today, I'll eat your shitty food, Herr Winkler. Tomorrow, I ram it down your fucking throat.'

He turned away, shouting through the hatch for the goulash. You could talk to Winkler like that, because it was the only kind of talk he understood.

In my mind, you see, I'd left already.

# FOUR

For so long I'd been afraid to think too loudly. That was East Germany's achievement. Wherever you spoke, they could hear you, whatever thoughts you hid, they could find them, if you planned or plotted or dissembled they could stare into your conscience and discern the guilt. I had helped them do it – so I knew.

I should have felt good stepping away that afternoon, knowing that my office would be closed or in chaos, knowing that my time – the little that was left here – was mine. But I didn't.

Crossing the road I was suddenly hot and clammy, despite the cool wind. For a moment I lost balance, swaying on the kerb, almost knocking into an old woman. One by one they came at me – all the symptoms that I'd known and watched for over so many years. The fear, the nervousness, the sudden disorientation.

I had never felt so trapped as on this my free afternoon.

Back to the park, I thought. But I took one look over the railings, saw the Glicks and thought better of it. Frau Glick was waving frantically at me and pointing to a carrier bag of food. But I didn't want company, didn't want their picnic – didn't want them.

As I walked away Glick caught up with me. 'What d'you think of it all, Herr Martin?'

He was wearing a beige, belted raincoat and a beret. Glick had been a war-baby, an orphan – the first generation to have been successfully brainwashed when the Communists came to power.

'I think it's wonderful,' I told him.

'But why?'

'Because people will be free to go where they like.'

He pondered this for a few moments.

'But what about the enemies of the State? There will be no defence, no control and . . .'

'I shouldn't worry, Herr Glick. There were never that many takers when it came to our little State.'

He blinked at me uncomprehendingly. 'But we have achieved so much. We have built a new system from the ruins of war. Of course there were mistakes and distortions – this has been admitted – but the party is reforming itself . . .' The voice died away.

I looked at him wringing his hands in despair. Glick was all right. He couldn't help swallowing it all in chunks, the propaganda, the false logic, the twisted tortuous manoeuvring of modern history. After all, he hadn't known anything else.

I touched his arm. 'It'll be all right. You'll be quite safe, and the family will be looked after. It's just a new approach, that's all.' For a moment I felt sorry for him. All his life he'd been lied to by the State. Now I'd lied to him once again.

I suppose Old Moore had always been my last resort. Steven Moore, of course, who got his nickname from the almanac and the fact that he'd been traitor longer than any of us.

I took the bus to the Prenzlauer Berg and walked the rest. Much darker now. And I felt better for having a purpose. Moore would know what to do. Moore the cheat, Moore the twister and turner. It took a man of those qualities to see things as they really were.

His door was open, the big brown padded door, that he had always kept locked. And it wasn't that the room was empty, but it was the little things which had gone missing that told me he'd left.

Left in a hurry too. In the kitchen the packet of cereal stood open on the table. The plate dirty in the sink, the tap still dripping.

Moore, why did you leave?

But I knew why. Even as I stood there I could remember the old father confessor, chatting away to us, back in the summer. He'd read the tea-leaves in Poland.

'All coming down now, chaps,' he had said to us, the little group of defectors who sometimes met on a Thursday, if they hadn't got a job or a woman or an invitation of any other kind – which mostly they hadn't.

'Jolly good thing too,' he'd added.

'What d'you mean?' Page had asked. He was the bad tempered bugger who'd sold MI5 down the creek after an affair with a waiter. 'How can it be good? This is what we bloody well came over for. Ideals, Communism. The bloody cause.'

'Excuse me,' Old Moore had said tartly. 'But if I recall correctly, you came over for a very different reason.' His eyes had twinkled and Page had fallen silent.

I sat down in Moore's favourite armchair. The picture of his wife had gone from the mantelpiece. She had died so young, and he had grown so old adoring her. The silver cup had gone too, the public school boxing trophy, and the signed photo of his meeting with Brezhnev that had stood next to it.

But, oh yes, I could still recall that conversation. Old Moore assuring us that Communism had been necessary to bring the two halves of Europe back together again, that it had all been decided in a secret East-West deal. That it was thanks to the likes of us that the borders were finally coming down and that freedom and true socialism would flourish.

I suppose we were all drunk at the time, otherwise someone would have told him to stop talking such cock.

But there were those who wanted to believe it. Not just Page, but Mason, the former head of Berlin station, and Kieran the archive man from the SIS, who never said much about anything except 'balls' or 'ridiculous' now and again. To them it really was an article of faith. Take it away and the whole house of cards would have fallen in on them.

And now Old Moore had gone, the first chance he'd got, after planning and arranging, and insisting point blank to all of us that he'd stay and see it through.

I couldn't really complain, I suppose, seeing that I'd lied as well.

Do you know what it is to be immobilized, to lose the use of your feet and the impulse to put one before the other? Normally, the books say, your motivation comes from things like love or duty, ambition, envy, hunger. But as I went down the list I couldn't seem to find them, sitting there, wondering whether Old Moore was getting pissed in a bar in West Berlin and having a bloody good laugh at our expense.

Who had he really been?

Who were any of us?

The caretaker threw me out. The old busybody had climbed the stairs without making a sound. 'He's fucked off,' he said superfluously, indicating some vague space that Old Moore might once have occupied. 'Fucked off without paying for next month. He's the second one to go.' He looked hard at me as if I might be the third. 'Like lemmings,' he muttered, turning to the wall and starting to giggle. I knew then he was drunk.

'Anyway,' he waved a fist at me, 'you can fuck off too – unless you want the place. In which case, pay me now.'

He retreated down the staircase and I followed his bald, shiny head, and the two scar lines on it, made, I hoped fervently, by some allied weapon.

You see, I'd had it with East Berlin, and its petty officiousness – the type of German who can embrace one kind of extremism after another and learn to love them all. The last forty years, of course, they'd done as they were told, buckled down, scrubbed their noses clean – and yet with a fear of them the old prejudices had lived on just below the surface. People like Glick and Dortmunder, always anti Poles, or Czechs or Jews – their hatreds as fresh and vivid as the day when the Iron Curtain came down.

Outside, the street echoed with noise. Teenagers were trawling through the puddles, some with bottles, some singing and calling, oblivious of the late hour.

'Pain in the arse kind of place,' Old Moore had once called it. 'But at least it's real, at least it's got principles, even if they're faulty.' I remember staring hard at his red bulbous nose and wondering why he sounded so plausible. 'Look at Britain,' he'd said, 'Britain under Thatcher.' And then he had sighed as if the effort of talking about it was too great. 'Not a value in sight, over there, not even on the horizon.'

And at that point I remember turning away from Old Moore's building, turning the same way the young people had gone, wondering why in the light of that awful neon streetlamp, a man was pointing a gun straight at me.

# FIVE

Looking back on it, there really wasn't time for fear. Or was it simply that everything about those early days was frightening? He made me get into the car first, and even with his hat pulled down over his face I could recognize him.

He slid in beside me.

'Herr Kirsch, is it necessary to wave a gun in my face?'

He looked embarrassed, and took off his hat, lending me a hand that felt like a wet herring.

'A thousand apologies, Herr Martin. But I had no idea whether you would wish to talk to me. You could have run away.'

'And you'd have shot me.'

'I . . . I . . . Of course not, Herr Martin . . .' And then much more quietly, 'I have never owned a gun before.'

'Where did you get it?'

'They are giving them out to us in case of reprisals. It is not clear how the masses will react.'

Oh yes, it is, I thought, and looking at his tiny, wizened features I wouldn't have given a lot for his chances, if a crowd of East Berliners got to know his real identity. Oskar Kirsch, rather senior official, in a rather little corner of State Security. The corner that dealt with people like me. Kirsch was like my old school prefect, without the misplaced sexual proclivities. Kirsch, my helper and my hinderer – my employer and guardian. At least a colonel, I thought, although he'd never told me.

He started the engine. His movements were jerky and his coordination was poor. And the car was unforgiving. The Trabant spluttered on to the main road, and we headed north, picking up speed. Kirsch was as familiar to me as the watery East German sausage they used to serve on the Alexanderplatz. Always a layer of grease on his forehead, thin metal spectacles housing his myopic eyes, and whatever the weather he would carry a three-quarter-length black leather coat – a hangover from Nazi days, to whose party his father had belonged.

'A source of great shame, Herr Martin,' he had once confided to me, attacking his nose with a handkerchief as if it were to blame for the paternal sin.

That was the delightful thing about Kirsch – and it was only delightful to me – his all-pervading insecurity. Every East German had it. You couldn't live cooped up behind a wall for thirty years without feeling someone was hiding something from you. But he seemed to have suffered more than most.

After all, he had occasionally been allowed over into West Berlin, with a few pfennigs to spend, his eyes no doubt watering with envy and greed. It would have been like a day trip to paradise only he could never admit it. I remember asking him what he'd bought. 'Herr Martin,' he'd said (we never did graduate to first names), 'the place was full of beggars. I felt it was my duty to share with them the little money that I had.'

I had known then what a lying little bastard he was. Kirsch would have kicked his own grand-mother in the guts, sooner than share some Western currency with her. But I hadn't been able to resist playing along.

'I expect the poor of West Berlin were awfully grateful to you.' I had said.

He'd looked at me and then nodded his head in agreement. 'You are right, Herr Martin, I also had this impression.'

I had gone on laughing about Kirsch for years, until the time when I had seen him beat one of his own defectors almost to death. And so now I didn't laugh about him at all. Not that night – nor on any other.

He was like so many outwardly bumbling idiots. They're vague and they're helpless until they locate the thing that turns them on. And then the mind is suddenly focused like a steel blade and they're frighteningly engaged and in control. Kirsch's speciality, camouflaged behind the silly, nervous little face, was violence.

I looked at him, clinging manically to the wheel. He was constantly worrying the car, changing gear when he didn't have to, over-revving, grinding on the brakes, and we were way out in the eastern suburbs that I didn't know at all.

'Where *are* we going?' I tried to sound unconcerned.

'A party, Herr Martin. A leaving party. No cause for you to worry.'

It was the most roundabout of routes, swinging us in a twenty-mile arc south into Potsdam. I knew the street, tatty, straight and grey, broken up by the tramlines that stopped suddenly before the Glienicke Bridge.

We got out and I could smell the fresh water from the Wannsee and the clean country air. Berlin could occasionally be a thing of beauty, although I didn't hold out a lot of hope for that night.

Kirsch led the way into a small red-brick block of flats, taking the stairs to the basement. Two men, evidently guards in civilian clothes, barred our way, and then saluted abruptly. Normally, it looks odd when people salute out of uniform. This time, it looked thoroughly unpleasant. An impression instantly confirmed as Kirsch opened the door and pushed me none too gently inside.

# SIX

And this is a bunker, I told myself. This is where they run.

God save me from those moments of panic, when strange doors open ahead of you and your life walks away on its own. I must have been holding my breath – and yet there was no panic here.

The room was about twenty foot square. Single lightbulbs hung from the open-brick ceiling, and along trestle tables, almost in formation, a dozen people were tapping at computer keyboards, peering at lines and letters on screens.

Oh, I knew them all right. Not by name or by face but by the discipline in their expressions, and the way they sat. These committed professionals, made in thousands by the German Democratic Republic, for use when needed. The final guardians of the system, the steel claw that would go on twitching long after the animal had died.

'This way, Herr Martin.' Kirsch gave a little bow.

Another door and a much smaller room. And you could tell it was the last stop on the line.

The man behind the desk was an older version of Kirsch, but his face had been violently re-arranged. The nose jutted out at a crazy angle, the cheek-bones seemed set on different levels. The dark skin was patterned with pock-marks. It was like a jig-saw puzzle assembled in the dark.

'Sit down.'

I became aware that Kirsch was no longer there – and that the door had closed behind me.

'Herr Martin, *ja*.'

I sat quite still.

The man poured himself water from a carafe on the desk.

'Herr Martin, Kirsch may have indicated . . .'

'He didn't.'

'I see.' He gulped more water. 'There is very little time, Herr Martin, so I will not waste it. You can see we are shutting down our operations for the time being.' He held up his hand as if he thought I'd talk him out of it. 'No, there is no going back.'

I cleared my throat. Some British habits never leave you. Like the need to be introduced. 'Who are you?' I found myself asking.

'Schmidt will do.'

'Someone came to my flat, Herr Schmidt . . .'

'This we know, Herr Martin.'

'Then you also know what happened to the man.'

'An unfortunate road accident . . .'

'Accident, Herr Schmidt?'

He got to his feet. Taller than I'd expected. Taller and wider. I shouldn't have argued.

'Herr Martin ... sometimes ...' He paused and then shrugged as if it were of passing interest. Truth one minute, lie the next. No barriers. No borders. He shook his head, as if grappling with an academic puzzle. 'I am unsure who carried this out, but it did not surprise me.'

'Why?'

'He was playing games.' Schmidt sat down again. 'These are bad days in East Berlin, OK? Wall comes down, people leave, the West takes over. New situation.' He rammed a forefinger on to the table. 'So what happens? State security collapses. Eighty thousand of us. And the world is told we are evil men.'

'What did you expect?'

'Expect, Herr Martin? We expected nothing.' He seemed to laugh but no sound came out. 'We were fully prepared for the chaos that is all around us. You see? You look at the streets? Discipline and order broken down completely – you like this, Herr Martin? Does it remind you of home, *ja*?'

'The man who visited me ...'

'What did he tell you, Herr Martin?' Schmidt's eyes had narrowed perceptibly. 'Did he offer you something, a trade perhaps, a little information? Maybe he even handed you a gift – something for nothing, a keepsake. People – some people – have been known to do such things.'

In that instant every alarm bell I'd ever heard began ringing inside my head.

'He gave me nothing.'

Schmidt kept on staring, as if trying to assess the value of my answer. 'It would not be clever to lie, Herr Martin, you realize, not this time, mm?'

I shifted in the chair, feeling my shirt wet against my back. The air was stifling. 'Where are we?' I asked.

'We are underground, Herr Martin. We used to be on top. Now we are underground.' This time he laughed aloud, not a false laugh. Not an effort. The amusement was genuine. 'Is this not a basement?' He stopped to wipe a tear from his eye. 'But we have nothing to do with political groups. The Communists and all their nonsense. They are already gone. Like farts in a storm, Herr Martin. We are no longer interested in the left or the right, or the politicians. None of that.'

He broke off and leaned back in the chair.

I let the silence widen between us. He drank more water, swirling it noisily around his mouth.

Of course, it occurred to me later, he must have practised this moment – my own Herr Schmidt, the man without a real name, the man in a Potsdam basement, ruling a little corner of East Germany while he still could. And, even then, I was prepared to write him off as a crank, to leave, to go back to my flat, to play my records, and think God knows what about everything for another day . . . only he

48

came round and positioned his face about an inch from mine, and I could smell power and sense danger, much as animals must do, out in the wild.

'Our interest, Herr Martin, is quite simple.'

And I knew then what he was going to say. 'Germany, Herr Martin. Just as it's always been. Germany.'

When he sat down again he was sweating freely from the excitement. He poured more water, his movements at once quicker and more certain. And now he was alive. Now he wanted to talk.

'Until a week ago, Herr Martin, I was a judge. Supreme Court of the German Democratic Republic.' There was a suggestion of relish as he pronounced the long words.

'And now, where can you go?'

His turn to be surprised. 'Why should I go anywhere?'

He smiled a few gold teeth at me. 'Herr Martin, I am to be a vital and trusted member of the new Establishment. It is true, I may not be able to practise as a judge, but only for a year or two. By then, whatever investigations are in progress will have ended.' He relaxed his elbows on the desk. 'No witch-hunts, Herr Martin. This has already been agreed. No more trials at Nürnberg. The Western powers have already agreed. And you know why, don't you, Herr Martin?'

I didn't answer, didn't want to interrupt the flow.

'It is because of their own actions, my friend. You think they didn't all play their own games over the last forty-five years. Trade unions, politicians from left and right, singers, writers – the list . . .' he pointed at me, 'the list of those from your country who came here and enjoyed themselves, took our hospitality, made their own deals and then went home to sit on the high moral ground.'

'I don't understand.'

'Perhaps, Herr Martin, you do not wish to understand . . .'

'Then tell me.'

Schmidt reached into a drawer of his desk and took out a file. It was grey and carried nothing more than a number, stamped on the front cover.

'Open it,' said Schmidt.

Inside was a list of British companies – some of them well known, but there were others that meant nothing to me.

'A list of participants, Herr Martin.' Schmidt sat back in his chair, looking immensely satisfied. 'Participants in a single operation. A trading arrangement, Herr Martin. The companies involved were of use to us and we were of use to them . . .'

'Which means?'

'I will tell you what it means. Each of these companies had trading relations with South Africa, at a time when this was forbidden by your government – and indeed by others. Under the arrangement worked out here in East Berlin the goods came first to us, and we despatched them to Africa with changed markings. We were the middle men, I think you say. We were paid a fee and we did as we were asked. Where Western currency was concerned, we had few scruples, if any at all.' He sighed and took another sip of water. 'There were times when I used to think we were more Capitalist than any of you.' He chuckled. 'And yet you knew nothing of these kinds of operation, Herr Martin? They were never talked about in your department?' A quizzical eyebrow lifted. 'No, but of course not.'

A thought occurred to me and I didn't find it pleasant. 'Why are you telling me this? I could perhaps use it in some way . . .'

'What way is that, Herr Martin?'

'There are people in the West . . .'

'Don't be naïve, my dear friend.' He looked at me pityingly as if I were a schoolboy, turning in poor homework. 'Who would listen to you? I tell you the West does not wish to further dirty its hands. It is what the Federal Republic has told us. No second-class citizens from the East, no recriminations. There is to be a spirit of pride and reconciliation. And no looking back. After all,' he sniffed loudly, 'we Germans have had enough of that.'

'You didn't answer my question . . .'

'Why am I telling you this? Let's just say that we might do some business together, Herr Martin. We

51

both have an unfinished problem – perhaps we can complete our tasks together.'

'I doubt it.'

'Really, Herr Martin. I do not.' Schmidt looked down at his desk. 'The man who visited you was a liaison officer between our service here in Berlin, and our fraternal allies in the Socialist world. Some of the information he possessed is in our files. Regrettably much of it was in his head.'

'That's too bad.'

'Bad for all of us, Herr Martin. My strong conviction is that he was killed by one of our sister agencies, possibly the KGB, because they feared he might give something away. After all, Herr Martin, new times, new alliances. Who knows what any of us will do now that the Wall is down.'

'You said, "bad for all of us".'

'My dear Herr Martin – the man comes to see you, he chats with you, he spends time in your flat. You say he gives you nothing, but how can we be sure. How can the people who killed him be sure? This is not good in our business, this kind of uncertainty.'

I didn't like the way the conversation had developed.

'Why did the man come to me at all?'

'This also, Herr Martin, is uncertain. But I do have a theory.' He paused as if expecting me to offer him money for it. 'One of the operations he worked on concerned information from a KGB agent working in London. A traitor in your former service. Someone they may have been wishing to protect, at this difficult time . . .'

'And your own interest in this?'

Schmidt sighed dramatically. And in that moment I was tempted to see him as just an old con man who couldn't and shouldn't be believed. For he was cruel and cold, and knew the game better than I ever had.

He leaned forward. 'Herr Martin, there is little love these days between former employees of State Security – such as myself, and the KGB. We find now that at each stage of the game they have betrayed us. When the riots were bad, they stayed home. When our leader was in trouble, they supported his opponents. It is they who have brought us down, Herr Martin. And you ask what is my interest in this.' He clenched his teeth as if he wished someone were caught between them. 'Our brothers in Moscow appear to be tidying up, Herr Martin. You would not wish to be tidied up as well.'

The voice was a whisper, but I heard every word.

Kirsch had come in. And before I realized it, we were pushing past the men at the computers, out on to street level, where the cold threatened to cut us down. And I was thinking, God they're desperate – the good old Stasi, who never lost a file, never forgot a name, prided themselves that they could lock on to any moment of your life they wanted, and destroy it. Now, they too had been betrayed and were looking for revenge.

'So, Herr Martin,' Kirsch smiled benignly as if he'd arranged the whole thing. 'A useful conversation, *Ja*?' His eyes were moving all over me but I hadn't expected what came next. It took away my breath, as much from shock as from the sheer pain as his fist slammed into my stomach, seeming to catch my insides, ripping and tearing as it went.

He was already walking away, and I was on my knees, marvelling through tears at the gratuitous violence – and the grotesque creature that performed it.

Maybe it was two hours, maybe three before I got back to the flat. I have chosen to forget. Such a joy it is when the mind can bury pain. And yet the hatred lives through it all – as much a driving force as any love, and far more certain and consistent. My hatred for Kirsch and anything that moved around him was what got me home. The walk, the drive in a truck, the walk again. The thought of what I would do to Kirsch in return, if life would only give me the chance.

As I entered the building, and the light came on in the hallway, I must have stopped and stared for several minutes. It was like a small corner of a photograph. You look at it, this way and that, trying to identify the whole.

And really it wasn't so difficult, for the black leather heap on the tiles became recognizably part of Frau Ansbach's frame, with the twisted high heels, and the laddered tights, face up with the python brooch snapping at her throat. And I wanted to ask her what in the name of heaven she was doing in the hallway, when I realized her head wasn't attached at the angle it should have been. I turned off the light because it wasn't helping either of us, and I knew then what I would do.

As I took the stairs up to my flat, two at a time, I could feel the cold on my spine, and my heart was thumping out the kind of urgent, irregular messages I hadn't heard for years. And, oh yes . . . I was running.

## SEVEN

Up until that point, only two moments of genuine despair had stood out in my life. Neither had anything to do with my safety.

The first occurred when I was fifteen. It was a summer afternoon and I was deeply asleep – almost coincidentally sitting in a physics laboratory at a boarding school in London. In those days I didn't do afternoons – the effort of staying awake after lunch somehow always seemed too great.

And you know when you're caught. That annoying hand on your shoulder, the admonishing tones, the warning to do better in future or else . . . And yet the teacher was standing over me – Mr Shepherd, I think – with at least something approaching a tear in his eye, and a kindly expression that I hadn't seen before.

He had, indeed, put a hand on my shoulder and was using it to lead me out of the classroom and along the street, while I hurriedly ran back through my list of current crimes.

And yet I felt a deeper sense of foreboding than on previous such occasions, and our shadows seemed long, traced out on the pavement, and our footsteps slower than they might have been, as we headed off to see the headmaster.

'I'll leave you here, boy, if that's all right,' Mr Shepherd had said when we reached the study door.

And inside, the headmaster was sitting at his desk, red-faced and flustered, with bad news to tell, and no fine way to tell it.

No elegant expression, though, could have prevented the brick wall that seemed to rise out of nowhere to confront me.

My father had died on the operating table, even as I had been sleeping in class. Dead of a stroke, so severe and so sudden that his life had ended with his mind unconscious, and me, just a mile away, unable to see him go.

How was it, I wondered, that the man who had given me life could fail, so spectacularly, to hold on to his own? I remember sitting down on the headmaster's sofa, aware of a sudden coldness that hadn't been there earlier.

'No need to go back into class,' the headmaster said. 'Only physics after all. Never my strong point.'

'I think I'll go to the hospital,' I said.

'Perhaps that'd be best,' he replied, shaking my hand in an effort to transmit his sympathy.

To be blunt – and I only say this after so many

years – Dad would have had to go sometime. That is, after all, the natural order of things. And maybe it's designed to strengthen you for all life's other tragedies. Only nothing, even that, could have prepared me for Cassie.

For whereas Dad had had the goodness and grace to leave my daily thoughts, only to return in memories of sunshine and happiness – Cassie never went away. Cassie is with me now. Cassie was there as I threw shirts into a holdall and looked unlovingly around that East Berlin flat. I took my old British passport and some West German marks from the drawer by the bed. And even at a distance of seven hundred miles and four years, I couldn't help wondering what she was doing at that same moment, as I prepared to alter my own life once again.

It wasn't just that she was American – she being open by birth, me being closed. Cassie had grown up with the endless Western sunshine – a planet away from the childhood I'd spent in a raincoat, walking dogs on blasted heaths.

A good climate, I now realize, frees you to think about other things, to stroll out with empty hands and open eyes.

Not to labour the point but my limpid upbringing did not prepare me for the way she would awake and seize a new day – hers to conquer, mine to endure.

To Cassie nothing ever looked the same twice. She would examine familiar objects with an air of such excited discovery that even I began to dry out.

Cassie, once Cassandra, leading with her charm. The narrow face and the wide eyes were long ago deemed beautiful to all beholders.

It had fitted, all of it. She, being at the US embassy in London, liaising with the Service over in Kennington. She, elegant and smiling as she expounded the interests of the Central Intelligence Agency to the four horsemen of MI6. They, who seldom said anything except, 'We're across that one' or 'We're taking that on board'. All purpose words, somewhere between everything and nothing.

At times, she used to say, it was like holding a seance to contact the living. Every so often she would shake them from their tree with nothing more than a human enquiry.

'Are you gentlemen having fun?' she had asked at the end of a meeting. Someone apparently began to dribble in shock. 'I mean do you really enjoy this?' And then she had caught the faintest of smiles in that coldest of all rooms and Cassie had known she was there. The mountain had moved. The way was clear.

Cassie why did you ever go?

The way I'm leaving now, fearful, hurried, with the ghosts drawing in around me.

I recall the feeling of hanging one-handed from the edge of the world when you walked out. Just as I had when Dad died – just as I felt now in the flat in East Berlin, once mine, already abandoned.

# EIGHT

Don't go through the hall. Not with her there. Frau Ansbach, dead on the doorstep of a new life.

Just when she would have begun dreaming of parties in the West, Coca-Cola on the Ku-Damm, the frills, the fripperies, the nonsense things on that side – and a fresh pool of men, still to be discovered.

I climbed through the first-floor window, on to the roof of the shed, down into the courtyard. There was light from the Glicks' flat, music from Dortmunder's and no one else at home, unless they were sitting in darkness, saying prayers for the future.

You couldn't see the full building to wish it farewell – just the crooked chimneys against the clouds and the frozen drains at ground level, and the bicycles belonging to the children Glick.

To me it had always seemed more like an asylum than a home. Special, surely, and all of us with our extra private histories that only the Mother State would ever know.

In our own ways we had all worked for Kirsch. I

know that now. Frau Ansbach, the most innocent, the part-time eavesdropper. Glick was something boring in records. Dortmunder, I suspected, was a campus informer. He did a little teaching at the Humboldt University, teaching and socializing and finding out who, exactly, went to the peace meetings in the churches, who had looked over the Wall too long and too hard. What would he do in the new era?

I shook my head. I wasn't going to miss them, but they were all I had known.

They had been my real education into the Eastern bloc – their prying, their pettiness, their humour, whispered, as schoolchildren so often do behind their hands in case teacher heard them.

I walked through the courtyard into the street. Most likely teacher Schmidt was still in his bunker, staring at screens, preparing to join the world he'd abused and spied on.

And now, Martin, it's reached you and you're scared to move. What an irony! You can't even cross the city without shaking and sweating and . . . look at your hands, wet inside the gloves, your mouth open, murmuring to yourself like a lunatic.

Face it Martin, poor, stupid Frau Ansbach is dead, the visitor is dead. People are dying around you in numbers that strongly suggest your own life expectancy is not that great. Tidying up, Schmidt called it. 'You would not wish to be tidied up as well.'

I turned down a side-street, and sat behind a low wall, invisible from the pavement.

I was running from East Berlin, but running in all probability into the arms of a traitor in London. And yet what did I know that made me a target? Who did I know?

I had to find out who was at the centre. I hadn't spent four lousy years in East Berlin for the greater glory of the KGB. People had to pay for the past. The bill was overdue. If there was no one else, I would have to make sure the account was settled.

It was taking time to work all this out. Too long away from the real world. Too long inside a sanitized cage with mirrors for walls and watchers beyond them.

Which brings us to the real question, Martin – maybe they really turned you. Maybe you've been so long in East Germany that you can't survive in the outside world. Don't tell me you really liked it – don't say it was easier not to have choices, easier to sit in your cage. Look at yourself, Martin – you got seduced by the routine, the certainties, the food in your stomach, the absence of a struggle. And they never asked much of you. A little spying on their fraternal allies – a note or two on personalities and their habits – suggestions on procedure. Oh God, maybe they caught you when you were weak, and made you weaker, made you theirs, a dependent, a client, with all your old values left on a shelf because they were too much effort to pursue. And that's the thing about Democracy – it's all about effort, Martin. Remember when you lived in one? You have to participate, speak out, engage. They require it.

Here they required nothing more than your silence and your presence. Be a zombie and that was wonderful. Don't go to the Wall, don't cross it. Don't think about it. Be a zombie, die a zombie and when the time comes you'll be sent off as a hero.

God it was easy to live in the East. And how comfortable just to kick against it in your mind – when you know damn well you won't do a thing against it.

Wonderful thing – the mental protest. Don't have to hit the streets, carry a banner, even shout a slogan. But inside your head, you're tearing the whole system to pieces. Fucking Communists, box-heads, I'll shake you buggers so hard . . . Dream on Martin, because those were the only battles you ever fought. Dream on.

I got up and walked on. Unter Den Linden was almost deserted. And as I passed the parliament buildings, hearing the echoes of thirty years non-sense and diatribe – I could see the triumphal arch, hard against the Wall – the Reichstag beside it,

West Berlin, like Disneyland somewhere over there.

Left on to the Friedrichstrasse. Mum, you walked this way when you went home that day, hurt, so very hurt and disappointed.

Nearly there – only a hundred yards to go – a hundred last steps. And you're going home Martin. They promised you that, didn't they? Only not like this, without a light of welcome in the window.

And it was only then that I reached inside my coat pocket, remembering my old British passport, still valid, handing it to the East German border guard, seeing my own wet finger marks on the blue cover.

A few more steps, along with the tourists and others – others! East Germans for God sake! How quickly they take it for granted, jumping over the Wall, jumping back.

Up to the little door. 'Go on,' someone said. 'Hurry it up.' Push it open and hand the book over once again.

And suddenly I realized this passport would be known to them, that it would be recorded as I crossed the checkpoint and that within an hour, maybe less, Herr Schmidt would be informed that I'd gone through. I could see his people slumped in their bunker over their computers, check-checking on a changing world – tracking me step by step.

I can't really recall the next few moments. The wind was so sharp and cold and the night sky unaccountably bright. I had visions of a few photographers, some soldiers in uniform, lights and signs and noises that were unfamiliar.

Two streets away, well inside the American Sector, I stopped in the doorway of a shop, put down the holdall and felt the sickness rising in my throat, racking my body in spasms – as if the poison of the last four years was coming to the surface.

When it was over, I sat in the gutter, shivering, with the tears welling up in my eyes.

'Going over', we used to call it. Only now I'd gone back.

I knew West Berlin from the old days when there were just angels and devils – long before they decided to intermarry and change all the rules.

At times, in my flat, I would close my eyes and dream of walking up the Ku-Damm, of decent meals and films.

Cassie had featured in those far-off fantasies, but never close-up. At times I would see her on the other side of a shop window, or in a moving car. There, but not there. Entering my life and then leaving it – just the way it had happened.

Eventually I got up and hailed a taxi to the zoo. I had money. In the Stasi, we'd all had that – the lovely marks from the West, paid each month as a portion of our salary.

To me the zoo was much more like a jungle, where you could live or die among the crowds, the neon lights and the incessant traffic. And no one would care which you chose.

But I couldn't help the sudden rush of excitement, couldn't stop myself buying the ultimate luxury of a beer and sausage from the nearest *Schnellimbiss*, standing back, laughing wildly like a thing demented, surely in that moment the luckiest man alive.

I found the Hotel Astoria, three streets along the Kantstrasse, partially re-vamped like me, cosy, *gemütlich*. And did the Herr need help with his luggage, and did the Herr require anything further that night?

And where do you begin?

But now I felt the West like a drug, coursing inside me. Suddenly I wanted to drink it in, hold it, breathe it, make it mine. I pushed past the porter, his hand outstretched for my bag. Two startled old women in the lobby seemed to gasp. And I took the steps two at a time. And I couldn't recall energy like this, the instant urgency gripping all my senses.

Maybe it was the empty room that stopped me — the characterless, airless, little rectangle, the shutting of the door behind me, the key in my hand. Something slowed me.

I put down the holdall and sat on the bed. It was softer than any I could remember. I took off my shirt and lay down. If the West, I thought, could only do something for me, would it stop the pain over my eyes and the sensation of being so utterly lost – just at the moment I thought I'd been found.

# NINE

If it hadn't been for Cassie McNeil I wouldn't have
been in the Astoria that night, or in my flat in East
Berlin, or any of the other mosquito-ridden hovels
I'd slept in over the last four years.

Not her fault, of course. But whose fault is it
when you connect and weave dreams that are
never realized.

We met at the worst of times, in the worst of
circumstances. The time when politicians stop
talking, the time when governments are rocked
deep below their foundations – an intelligence
fiasco, never reported, never acknowledged, the
whispers and rumours about it buried in unmarked
graves.

It never went public and never will – the loss of
the largest network we'd ever run inside East
Germany, picked up and broken systematically
piece by piece, human being by human being. To
those who knew there was no comfortable cathar-
sis. No funerals where you expunge your own
guilt, and comfort the bereaved, and take refuge in
the ceremonies and procedures with which society

helps us all on our way. None of that. For this was such a startling and inexplicable failure, such a momentous act of betrayal that the intelligence machine halted and stuttered and broke down by the roadside.

It was the event that was to bring about my so-called defection to East Berlin. It was to bring me Cassie McNeil and wrench her from my grasp.

News of it had come as I was unwrapping my lunchtime sandwich and I can remember it was cheese and tomato in a sesame bun . . . funny what you recall when tragedy breaks. Maybe the mind simply takes refuge in trivial details, hiding from the daylight.

They sent me in a taxi to the American Embassy because the pool driver had gone out for his lunch. I was to be the advance messenger, awkward and ill-informed – my instructions to summon the US Intelligence chiefs to an emergency session and warn them that this one was 'cosmic'.

Cassie had greeted me on that most awful of days – cool in her yellow summer dress and black high heels. 'Why don't we look on the bright side,' she'd advised, taking in the full range of my discomfort.

Understandably she was the only one to look on the bright side – and she too mislaid her sense of humour once the full extent of the disaster became known.

Twenty-six agents and couriers, variously

mislaid, arrested or disappeared in unpleasant circumstances, across East Germany. And what could be more unpleasant than that? An entire post-war network – the high-level and low-grade all at once. The most devastating knee in our groin.

It must have been around seven when we left the Embassy. 'I haven't got any plans,' she said. And nor had I. Besides I wanted to be with someone who could share the awfulness of that day. Together we carried it out across the city, through the groups of unsuspecting tourists and the theatre-goers of the West End, and the people who had never even heard of the network and never would.

We walked in silence for maybe an hour, leaving the sound effects to others . . . Hyde Park was just a single crowd. By Victoria it had thinned and along Birdcage Walk I felt the first breeze of the day, watching the dark-suited arms and legs of government, swinging home to the suburbs.

There, in sight of Big Ben, she took hold of my arm, tightly, purposefully – and I knew she was thinking the same.

For she too had worked Berlin in those far-off times. She had probably known Fischer and Pedrich, or a few of the others. She would have known just how much they'd cared, how much they'd believed in causes that now seem so out-dated and so scarcely imaginable.

All those fairy tales about tunnels under the Wall, about the no-man's land and the scatter guns

– about fighting the most intrusive dictatorship the world had ever known.

But that day in summer we had no idea what was to come. Our thoughts focused on the present – shattering as it was – and the men and women who wouldn't get to see that future.

'It'll never change,' I had said to Cassie. 'Not in our lifetime, not in the one after us either.'

And she had nodded, and we had walked on, closer with each step, to one another.

We had met again the next day and the day after that, and when the weekend came, and we rested our fears and our consciences, it seemed natural that we'd be together. Time became Cassie's time, often late and haphazard. For in her life, dates were only ever approximate, the caveats already written in, the alterations taken for granted.

In those days, I don't know why, we went out instead of staying in. Perhaps I do know – we weren't twenty any longer, and there isn't the same compulsion to wolf your food. You can wait for the main course, wait until it comes to you, in a time of its choosing.

And yet, even then, Cassie brought to my world an outer sparkle and inner intensity that I had not thought existed.

I remember calling round for her one Sunday evening. She answered the downstairs intercom and buzzed open the lock. On the third floor, her own flat was open, the hall and the sitting room empty.

'It's me,' I shouted.

I heard her laugh from the bathroom. 'I wonder what gave me my first clue.'

For a moment there was a nervous silence. And it's always when you stop talking that you say the most.

I glanced round the flat, seeing the clock on the mantelpiece, the same chairs and curtains and . . .

'You can come in here, you know. If you want to.'

Had I misheard? And yet there was something new in the voice, an intonation she hadn't used before.

She was sitting up in the bath, the water lapping over her knees. The Cassie I'd dreamt of knowing.

'You can get in,' she told me. 'Only you have to promise not to look.' It was the only promise she ever asked of me.

There began for me a collection of days and nights, that I have bound in gold in my memory, an anthology of elation and intensity that I had not believed I would ever find.

For she took me back inside my own mind, re-modelling the world as I had known it. She could tease away my anger, she could direct my energy. In a single day I lost count of the occasions when her words or actions would draw me to her, ever tighter and more secure.

And yet, whether in illusion or reality, it was I who took charge. I who planned the future, who offered comfort and reassurance, who held her, as so often she would cover her chest with her arms, like a child, seeking strength and comfort around her.

My own need was simply to care for her and provide her with a springboard for her own fulfilment. For being American, she had reached her mid-thirties with both her dreams and ambitions still intact. Being Cassie, she needed to be given the freedom she sought.

Sometimes, she would return from her office, upset and frustrated by the internal politics – the White House in microcosm, she would say. Personnel were divided into the loyal and the untried. There were inner and outer circles. Dinners you got invited to, dinners you didn't. You could score your own rating, she said, by the parties you went to.

And I would take her hand and run down the long list of her achievements, as I knew them. We would recall her triumphs and her insights. We would plan strategies and discuss policies, aware somehow that we were covering distances together – that were denied us when we were apart.

Not that this was an intellectual relationship – it was simply a meeting of minds – and bodies. And the days when we got drunk and went to bed, or stayed sober and didn't get up, were just as valuable.

'There's so much there,' she would say. 'The things we know about, as well as the things we don't. The way our minds seem to operate together, without effort or trouble. You make me feel good about myself.'

I laughed.

'Why do you laugh? Don't you feel good about yourself?'

'It's not a concept we ever discuss in Britain.'

'Why not?'

'Well for one thing – look at the weather. How could we possibly get up in the morning and feel good about anything, let alone ourselves? National character. We feel lousy about everything, but we try to make use of that feeling. Creative energy. You know what I mean. The funniest jokes always come from the sad and downtrodden. The best art. We may be miserable but we *are* creative.'

I took her home once to meet Mum. No woman's woman my mother. And yet I could sense in the early minutes of their meeting that Cassie was a success. My mother, like everyone who met Cassie, began to enjoy her – the smile, the warmth, the quick wit.

We had gone there for tea, to the big London house, off Cricklewood Lane, with the wine-red carpet, and the old dog hairs which would never all come out. On the mantelpiece were the family photos that I could see Cassie studying, and wondering over – the shot of Dad, just a distant silhouette on a holiday mountain, me refusing to smile, my stubborn jaw recorded in less than lovely photo-colour.

At six o'clock I had looked at my watch, but Mum wouldn't let us leave. She hurried away to 'fry something up' for us amid the ancient pans and carrier bags that littered the kitchen.

'Do you cook at all?' she shouted to Cassie.

'I'm very good with an orange,' came the reply, and I could hear my mother laughing with pleasure.

A day later I called to thank her for the meal.

'Quite a girl,' she told me.

'You never said that before . . .'

'You never brought someone like that home before,' she countered.

There were, now that I look back, days when we didn't laugh much at all. At work it was the season for crucifixions. Each section was dredged and sifted and as ever, if the light shines brightly enough the cracks will appear. Some matter, some don't but they were determined to follow them all.

Daily, it seemed, there were casualties from the middle rank. We, the traditional blame-carriers, we who had failed either to give instructions or heed them.

My ancient friend, Clark, fitted the bill. We had attended the same ancient school, but in different classes. His sin – that he had liaised directly with the Berlin station – and seen nothing coming. He hadn't read the tea-leaves, they said. He hadn't looked inside the cup. Perhaps he didn't even have one. He had come to work on a Thursday morning to face the Committee and left that evening with a note about his pension.

Old Clarky.

Of course they used the disaster to settle scores, to re-arrange the furniture, re-upholster the place. A bit of blood-letting never did any harm. That was the wisdom of the day.

And yet they were really just scrabbling around. If rainbows lead to a pot of gold, treachery leads to a hall of mirrors, full of strange lights and distortions. Sometimes you see faces and shadows, glimpses of a fast-moving figure. But for the searcher there is only one constant – the image of himself, lost and uncertain, staring back in the reflections.

They gave plenty of warning before calling us in. I knew ten days ahead of my own 'appointment'. Doctor will see you Monday morning at ten. Their way of opening your pores, seeing what came out.

And I couldn't prevent the trickle of despair that seemed to drip its way into my life, poisoning as it went. It grew daily inside those government offices, with the green carpets and the grey filing cabinets, full of the stories of all those grey little lives that we'd lost.

I was going to make it, though. Determined

about that. With help from Cassie. She, who refused to complain, refused to throw rocks at the sky.

Of course, they put her through it. And being American there were more electronics and psychology and long words, instead of the vague British, 'Let's have a chat old boy' that often turned out to be an invitation to your own hanging.

In that period there was often hurt around her eyes, and I realized the pressure from the American end was growing. She became less inclined to discuss it.

'Look at it this way,' she'd say. 'You're in the basement or the penthouse. There's nothing in between.'

And about us?

'This is beautiful,' she said once, taking my hand, prizing the fingers apart, pushing her own inside. 'It's so unconditional, so free, so devoid of restraints and restrictions.'

I let that go round my head for about a minute.

'What d'you mean?' I asked finally.

She was still smiling. 'Well, we just have a good time, we don't expect anything from each other, we don't have to put on any sort of act . . .'

'And if we did?'

'If we did what?' A frown built itself into her forehead.

'If we did expect something?'

'Well,' she removed her fingers from my grasp. 'Then it would be different, wouldn't it?'

I seem to remember we were along the Embankment at the time – the South Bank Promenade – the end of a glorious evening in bed, in a restaurant, in step. And yet the urge to shoot myself in the foot seemed almost irresistible.

I stopped and turned to look at her. 'Let me get this straight. Are you saying this whole thing with us isn't as serious as I think it is? I mean, is this some kind of game for you?'

Oh God! Even now I can hear the voice – a petulant little schoolkid, pretending to be a man.

'OK!' She too had stopped. 'OK!' She was going to say something but stopped herself.

'What were you going to say?'

'It doesn't matter. Forget it.' Cassie tried to smile, but the expression was a lot colder than the river.

'Tell me,' the little boy whined on.

'I think I want to go home . . .'

'I'll take you.'

'I want to go by myself.'

That night I was angry at myself for letting her go, angry at her too because she had left me unhappy and desperate.

I didn't know it then but I'd begun to treat her like a drug. See her in small or large doses and the effect would be magnificent. One Cassie before bedtime and again in the morning. Just what I needed. Only if you want to continue like that you should buy a bottle of pills.

She must have sensed it. She didn't call me the next day, and I was still angry and didn't call either. And so a day passed without Cassie – a day I regretted so far into the nights of East Berlin.

# TEN

Over there, I had always woken myself. Here, on the first morning in the West, the city woke me. Its cars and trucks and trains – the sounds of people with challenges to face, lives to enrich – instead of the pompous, tacky little sham that we'd all helped to perpetuate in the name of the people.

I'd left the curtains open and now I couldn't help letting the anger in. Anger for the four years I'd spent crawling behind a wall.

'Settled in, have you?' They had kept asking for the first few months. Settled in! I hadn't even settled my backside in East Berlin, let alone anything more meaningful. Settled in? Of course, Herr Kirsch. Finally my life has a purpose, Herr Kirsch. Why did I not see the error of my ways years ago?

On one level it had been easy to string them along. Press their buttons, recite their lines. But they never let it go at that. They always checked, probed, questioned. That was their way.

I re-packed the holdall and went down to breakfast. In the dining room there was whispered conversation, a sprinkling of German formality, waitresses in black, swishing skirts. West Berliners – and I wanted to notice every detail, from the expensive make-up to the quiet confidence, to the shoes that were shiny, to the effort and trouble they'd invested to face the day.

Move it, Martin, don't daydream.

*Danke*. And that's for the service. Some of them looked at me as I got up. Well, I didn't fit the norm, did I? Not a tourist, because the clothes weren't casual enough. Not a businessman, because the hair was just too long and the blazer too old, and the cut too poor. So when I thought about it, there was nowhere else I could have come from – except the big, bad East. And the Astoria wasn't used to that. Not then.

At reception I asked for the bill. The clerk was in black morning coat and striped trousers, and he frowned at the computer print-out, as if it contained bad news.

'You wish for a copy, Herr Martin?'

'I wish to pay,' I corrected him.

The clerk sighed. 'One moment please.' He disappeared into a back room, returned seconds later. The frown had not gone away.

'A slight misunderstanding, I believe.' He coughed politely into a half-clenched fist. 'It appears the account has already been settled. A gentleman, I'm told, came this morning and paid. What time was that, Peter?' He turned abruptly as another clerk emerged from the back.

'A little after seven.'

'So, Herr Martin. As you can see, there is nothing to pay.' He smiled the kind of smile hotel staff reserve for stupid foreigners. 'You are luckier than you thought. No?'

I can't recall if I hid my feelings. The fear came first. Just reflex, pure, unfocused and all-embracing as I pictured Schmidt and his underlings, organizing this little demonstration, stretching out beyond the Wall, even as their system fell apart.

So they wanted me to know they were right beside me. The Stasi was with me. Such a comfort. Reassurance or pressure. The way they played the game, it could be either.

On the street outside, I stood close to the hotel wall – briefly unsure of the way to the station. Down the street by the Kempinski, a long line of black cars had assembled. The passers-by wore leathers and furs and colours, and the only grey was me.

A sudden image hit me of this figure in his shapeless overcoat, his hair flapping in the wind, life in a holdall. A man naïve enough to believe he was running. It was the reflection in a shop window on the morning that I had so wanted to celebrate – the morning they'd taken from me.

Of course in West Berlin, I was right in the middle of the new Europe – and yet the old one wouldn't let me go.

*     *     *

Looking back, it was that moment when I stopped running. They knew where I was and where I was going. The scope for independent action seemed limited. And in any case I wasn't the same sure-footed fellow who'd left the West four years before.

The man from the pleasant middle-class suburbs of London. Standard Brit. No really strong beliefs in anything, because none of them had ever been tested. And yet, in those days, I had taken chances and enjoyed it. Now it was different.

All right, I told myself, you've lived with lies and made them your home. And one day, you always knew it would end. But I hadn't had time to imagine Western life in 1989. Didn't know the issues, the talking points, the worries and the pressure points.

At Tegel airport I felt a stab of alarm when the immigration officer photocopied my passport. But I watched as he did the same with everyone. And nobody's free, I thought. Nobody comes and goes as they please.

You can easily get to the state I was in then – where everything worries you, and each new step worries you more.

They gave me a window seat, and an elderly nun sat next to me like an unwanted conscience. She reached for a boiled sweet from her bag and offered it to me and I took it, hoping there wasn't a price tag, that we wouldn't have to talk and get to know each other and that I'd have to lie to her as well.

But she shut her eyes as they revved the jets and I waited to feel the exhilaration of leaving Berlin, fully expecting my worries to be left behind on the ground. Only it never happens the way you think.

Passing through the low clouds I could still see Schmidt in the bunker, his eyes half-closed from fatigue. Even now, with the borders down, he was directing me on an operation I had to accept. You shouldn't be surprised, I told myself. When they lifted the lid on Eastern Europe all the slugs began crawling out, the filth, the lying, the double standards.

Only this was something more sinister.

We had levelled off way above the clouds, in a blue sky that would stretch, they promised, all the way to London.

# ELEVEN

I didn't see much of that sky. For the tiredness and the anguish came at me, in the jetstream over Germany, forcing me back against the seat, closing my eyes, pushing me under.

I knew that in London there was a whole box of memories I hadn't touched in years – and I didn't want to open it then. Yet I couldn't help extracting a single dog-eared recollection – the row with Cassie, the moment, all those years ago, when her life had walked away from mine, the moment to which I always traced my misfortunes.

Oh, I had called her in the end. And we had met and talked, but, in her eyes, the sparkle had gone – as if she had wanted and believed us to be perfect – and now she'd changed her mind.

And I recall thinking, how can I get inside your head? How did I hurt you? Where is that tiny, delicate nerve where you hide your hopes and your dreams? How can I mend it?

Then came the last supper. She waited until coffee before taking my hand. And the plates were cleared away, along with all the polite little pleasantries we'd exchanged over them.

Cassie sighed – and hung her head, and there was the 'now-to-business' expression that I'd only seen before in the Embassy.

She had said the words – all about having some time apart, and seeing how things worked out, and how she'd always be there for me, and I could call her when I wanted and . . .

For a few moments, sitting there at that table, I hadn't been sure who she was. And I was still wondering as she got up and touched my shoulder and walked away.

Words. But whatever they were, I was sure they couldn't change the situation. I realize now that something in me had found a home with Cassie, something well away from my will or desire. And the words couldn't alter it.

I was strangely calm. I ordered another bottle of wine – and I even managed to reflect on my impending 'little chat' with the section, just two days away. But I drank that wine, drank it down like so much lemonade, telling myself that nothing could touch me, nothing could take Cassie away.

Dreams. Alcohol has always done that for me.

The restaurant was in Knightsbridge – probably still is – and from there I drove into the park, heading North towards the Edgware Road, and the flat in Maida Vale. And I remember distinctly that my confidence wasn't holding. I couldn't kid myself about Cassie. She was too deeply inside my life, too strong a preoccupation. She was a central, pivotal component, and you couldn't remove it without paying a price.

It was late. There wasn't much traffic, but quite a few people were on the streets. And I remember distinctly the lights of an Italian restaurant as my final hard vision, before the drink seemed to wash me away. My jaw froze, and for a moment I felt separated from the car. I think I shouted Cassie's name again and again, and the pain of that evening and the alcohol seemed to be merging at terrible speed into a fatal concoction.

I suppose I saw her from some distance away – a young girl in a pure white dress, silhouetted against the dark buildings. For some reason she mesmerized me – and in that moment I wanted nothing more than to go up to her, and talk to her – some vision out of the night, something simple and innocent.

In the end, all I can do is repeat what I told the police – that I just needed the woman's help, that I needed her advice, that somehow, there was a chasm and a longing that had suddenly opened up in my life and I didn't know what to do. And it was only when the vehicle boarded the pavement, and the screams came to me through the windscreen that my foot hit the brakes.

Even after that, I couldn't see the girl in the white dress, not from where I was sitting, not where she was lying, halfway along the Edgware Road, a few minutes after midnight.

Fenton got me released about ten hours later. I don't know what he told the police, but presumably there are channels and forms – the sleight of the official hand. For suddenly we were outside Paddington Green police station with the morning traffic going mad on the Westway and the noise quite indescribable.

I only remember what he said to me: and it wasn't, 'What a stupid fucker, how could you have brought the service into disrepute?' and all the awful claptrap that I had expected and deserved. Instead he took me to a coffee bar off Lisson Grove.

I was cold, and my mouth was dry. Beyond the window pane autumn had arrived in dull, pale colours, with a strong breeze and an air of miserable resignation.

'I'm awfully sorry,' he muttered, pushing a mug across the white melamine. 'Could have happened to any of us, really.'

'But I still don't know what did happen.' I remember trying to raise the mug to my lips, but my hand was shaking too much and so I put it down again.

'Tell you what,' said Fenton, 'Why don't you come back to my place. We'll talk it over in peace and see what's best to be done.'

At the time, of course, it didn't occur to me that

there were many options. I would go to court, I would go to jail, I would never again get to hang my hat in the Intelligence community. People would click their teeth and shake their heads if my name ever came up. As we left the café and got into Fenton's sports car, I was convinced I was finished.

And over the next few hours, in his quiet, reassuring way, Fenton did his best to foster that view. I now realize that he attempted to kill me with kindness. He was like the preacher who visits a condemned man in the final hours before his execution.

'Is there anything you want?' he asks. As if there's really something he can get you. Like a plane out of there, a pardon, a fast car and the freedom to head for the hills.

So it was with Fenton – 'Make yourself at home,' he would say, adding later, 'We may not have long,' or, 'I'm not at all sure that we can stave this thing off. Ah well, live for the day.'

And I would watch him, grateful for the tone of comfort, with no idea where he was leading me.

Ironically it was Fenton who had been scheduled to chair my 'little chat' with the section. Fenton was section chief – known more familiarly as 'red leader' because of his hair colour. He was just two years older than me and much more clearly in the fast track. And try as I might I couldn't really dislike the man. For he wasn't that smooth, or good-looking, not even that experienced – and yet he possessed unerring intuition, combined with simple common sense. And that's all Intelligence ever was.

Fenton lived on his own in a mock Georgian terrace in Islington – Theberton Street, or Bickerton Street, something like that. It's a suburb much beloved of rich socialists – full of once-lovely houses in tatty streets, where the modern left-wing conscience can sleep easy and unenvied.

Yet here there was no sign of politics, no sign of the bachelor-zealot. Instead, it was a house with natural warmth, to which Fenton had added his own. Prints from Old Washington – where he had once been attached to the Embassy, a dark green carpet overlaid with Turkish rugs, books and papers in the kind of semi-discipline that only elderly cleaning ladies can impose. Fenton was in good shape.

Only I wasn't.

I must have slept for most of that day. There are dim memories of staggering down the steep, narrow staircase in the late evening, knocking on the door of the drawing room and seeing Fenton hunched over his desk, with a single lamp to illuminate his papers – in the same way I had seen my father, all those years ago.

We went into the kitchen and he warmed up soup from a can. I recall seeing that he wasn't good with his hands. He hadn't got any of the practised, perfect little gestures that some single men seem to cultivate. He fiddled ineffectually with the gas ring, and the soup was overcooked when he ladled it, lumpy and frothy into the bowl.

'If it's lousy don't suffer,' he said, smiling thinly.

I dipped a spoon into it. 'Not bad. In fact pretty bloody good, I'd say.'

'All right for prison fare . . .' he stopped himself. 'God, sorry. What a tasteless thing to say. I didn't mean . . .'

'Quite all right.' I could feel the redness spreading out over my cheeks. And yet Fenton had only spoken the truth. It would have to be faced. Now was as good a time as any.

'Why don't we go back to the sitting room?' he suggested. And I followed the old blue cardigan through the hall, over the brown and white tiles into a chair that seemed to sink forever, matching my mood.

He talked first. All about the section and some of the characters in it – the disaster over the East German network. God, the government was furious, the Permanent Under-Secretary was drinking himself silly in his office, files were leaving Archives to all and sundry. What a mess.

Fenton had been staring at the curtains and then he turned towards me, half his face in darkness.

'So who are we looking for?'

The question was so unexpected that it seemed to slice right into me, taking my breath away. In truth,

I hadn't thought of a traitor, let alone an East German since before ... but of course Fenton knew that, knew that my guard was down, that I was under exceptional duress, and that he had in his hands something as close to a defenceless victim as he was ever going to get.

He must have read the realization in my eyes ... for he got up to refill my glass, attaching a smile, mumbling something about what a good brandy he had in the cupboard, saved for a special occasion.

'Maybe you're tired,' he added. 'Long day. Better we talk tomorrow. Things'll seem clearer then ...'

By then, though, I felt quite calm and I told him, 'We can talk now, if you wish. After all, this *is* on the record ...'

Fenton didn't move, didn't react. But he knew what I meant. I looked round the room, realizing then that the warmth wasn't from him at all. He'd have called in the Service designers, the Service psychologists, and between them they'd have built the semblance of a home – relaxed, comfortable and completely false. Ideal place for a 'chat'.

He was standing beside the drinks cabinet. 'We don't have to get worked up about this ...'

'I didn't think we were.'

Fenton poured himself a whisky. It struck me that if he'd been older he'd probably have handled it better – either playing the nice guy or the grand intimidator – but he didn't seem to know which he wanted.

'Perhaps,' he said, 'perhaps events in the section were depressing you. I can quite see how they would. That's all I wanted to say. Maybe you just had your mind on other things, and that's how the accident came about.'

'Maybe.'

'And what about the section?'

'I don't know.'

Fenton smiled, but there was no sense of enjoyment. 'You don't know. I see.' He sat back and crossed his legs. 'We lose our whole fucking network in East Germany, you're one of the men running that desk – and you just don't know. You don't have a theory, a suggestion, an idea – nothing, right?' He smacked the cushions on the sofa. 'Why don't you just go to bed and think pretty damn hard about it. Because when I get up in the morning, I want some answers.'

I could hear his footsteps on the old staircase, shaking the wooden beams, closing the one door that he'd seemed to be holding open.

Fenton must have gone out early, because I heard the knocking on the front door and for a long time, I stayed where I was, thinking he'd answer it. In the end I pulled on one of his old dressing-gowns and opened the door, expecting an angry milkman or a special delivery, or something else of no relevance to me.

And she just stood there, trying to smile, as the

cool morning air swept past me into the house. But I couldn't help pulling her close, feeling my tears working their way out. Cassie what are you doing here? How did you find me? What a sight it must have been as the men and women of Islington shuffled past us to work.

'I can't stay. I'm not supposed to be here at all.' She came into the hall bringing life and colour with her. She wore a bright blue leather jacket and a dark skirt and the fresh, sweet smell of her untroubled world. 'I just wanted to say how sorry I was about the accident . . .'

'Don't think about it . . .'

'How can I not?'

'It's nothing to do with you. I was tired. Too much to drink. I lost my concentration.'

She took my left hand, holding the fingers tightly. 'I don't know when I'll see you again. They're putting a cordon around you. I don't know what's going on. Early this morning there was a call to the Embassy. You're out of bounds, untouchable. We're all to stand clear.'

And all I could feel was the pressure of her hand.

'I found out you were here and waited till Fenton left. I'm so sorry about everything.'

In a minute I would have to let go that hand, cast off the line . . .

'I better go. Try not to worry. Call me if you can.'

The hand was pulling away, and I could see that mass of thick, curly hair . . . for a moment she turned and looked at me without speaking. The eyes halfway between brown and black, telling me the saddest story of my life.

Cassie, would you say it before you go? You know the words – the three that teenagers slur and giggle over. Just so I can hear them and hold them and play them over to myself with your cadences and your mouth around them. A keepsake for the future. Not so much to ask.

But she couldn't say them – not on demand, because she was far too honest and genuine and if she did ever say them – they'd come with all the truth and sparkle the world could offer. One day, I have told myself, she'll say them to my face.

No day in history could have shattered a single man, like that one. I see Fenton returning, with his head down, and a slow, heavy walk. I hear him telling me that the girl in the white dress had finally died of her appalling car injuries, and that I was to be charged with manslaughter. I never questioned it.

He sits me down and what I can't remember is the pain that I felt, because the mind won't replay it. Part of the safety mechanism that's supposed to help us survive.

He tells me that there is a way out of it. They'd been planning it, just after the network had been blown. It's what the Service wanted from me – and what the country needed. Go in, he says, turn yourself over, work for them for a few years, and then cross back over the Wall, and tell us what you've got. Be a sleeper, but also be a mole. Burrow and dig. Get under their skin. Then steal their jewels and bring them back.

I must have said yes, or maybe I simply nodded. For I had no further resistance. And if they'd told me to clean cars in the street I'd have gone and done it.

But what I do recall is the figure in a black trenchcoat, checking that same night into a West Berlin hotel close to the Friedrichstrasse, waiting till three in the morning, then taking his bag along the wet, tarmac streets, the Wall on his left, skirting the puddles, hearing nothing but his own footsteps in the silence of the morning.

Bright lights then from the East, through the electric gate at the checkpoint, and the guards, armed and oh-so-sceptical, and the door shutting behind me to the West, and all the life that I'd ever known.

What had I done, I asked myself, that night, and for so many that came after?

We were descending into London in thick cloud, and yet I knew we were close to the ground. The jets were screaming, the undercarriage was down, the wings wiggled in the slipstream as the pilot straightened on final approach.

And now you're back, Martin. You came back

alone, just as you left. Only this time you tread with the greatest care in the world. Take it slowly, open your eyes. Lead the traitor away from his cover and his safety, from his friends and colleagues, from the two secret worlds which have fed his treason and his ambition.

Kill him before he can kill you.

# TWELVE

'Hallo, I'm back.'

'There you are! I knew I hadn't seen you for a while.'

'Four years actually. Nearly five.'

'My God, is it that long? Been somewhere nice have you?'

'East Germany.'

'What's the weather like over there?'

As I stood in line at Immigration I could imagine the conversation in the office. I'd just walk back through the door, and Sharon, my deeply untrustworthy secretary, would be in the same place I'd left her, plotting and scheming to become the Queen of the Pool.

Only I couldn't just walk in again. The Wall was down, but the door hadn't opened. You came home without permission, Martin, they'd say. You neglected your duties. In at the kill, like that, and then you leave before the funeral.

'Thank you, sir.' The voice of the immigration clerk. And I hadn't heard that in a while. Not the 'thank you' and not the 'sir' either.

I made my way to the carousel, while the loudspeakers announced a baggage handling delay and a pay dispute. A flash of anger hit me for all the wastage and complacency, and the luxury of even having such disputes – something they'd never tolerated in the East.

'You look a little lost.'

I turned to see the diminutive nun, standing almost directly beneath my armpit. She had that pale, scrubbed look that comes from purity within, but I couldn't help noticing the expensive spectacles.

'I was going to say something on the plane, because you seemed so nervous, but you slept all the way.' So matter-of-fact in her Irish brogue, almost as if we knew each other. 'Is everything all right?'

I wanted very much to tell her the truth, that nothing was all right, and I wasn't just nervous, I was terrified of what I had to do. But she couldn't have helped.

'I'm tired. That's all,' I told her. 'Not a great traveller.'

Somehow she trailed me out to the line of taxis, chatting about the Mother Superior and the joy of travel. And shouldn't we thank God for such a beautiful morning, young man.

And even to me, numbed and anxious, that seemed a little excessive. Since by then it must have been four in the afternoon, and I hadn't been anyone's young man for a very long time.

But I was already stepping towards the taxi. Maybe I was two paces from the door handle, maybe three, what does it matter? The moment I reached out, the taxi behind slammed straight into the back of my vehicle, its horn went off and a dozen rapid-fire expletives were let off into the atmosphere.

I remember turning to look at the damage, and then wondering what my driver would do about it. But even as I glanced towards him a huge cobweb crack appeared like a fatal incision across the windscreen and I heard myself gasp in shock, as the glass shattered inwards. Seconds later I was aware of a woman screaming, somewhere above me, because I was hugging the ground, arms over my head, the most useless protection of all. As I sat up, I could hear sirens – and only then did I get it. Only then did I see the men in their plain blue uniforms and flak jackets, revolvers in their hands, shouting orders, running towards the terminal exits.

Get out, Martin. Get out.

And I pulled myself up against the railings of the walkway – and for a brief instant took in the wounded taxi, its driver slumped in the front seat, blood everywhere. More screaming and the glass all underfoot, and so many men with guns drawn . . .

And I wasn't used to this kind of thing. In East

Berlin they never liked attacks in public, unless *they* organized them, and I could understand why. It doesn't foster respect for authority if people are lying on your streets with head injuries, if your tourists start panicking and calling for their assorted embassies, and schoolchildren scatter in shock like frightened rabbits. All of which was happening around me.

But I was running now – past the bus stops and the meeting points – and I didn't stop till I reached the main road. At the intersection the security cordon was already going up. A pair of ambulances chivvied through the dawdling traffic, a police helicopter was landing on the grass verge, the image of an angry monster woken from a deep sleep.

This early evening in London.

Across the road was an airport hotel, and I sat myself in the quiet and clinical little lobby with the piped music – and a song I hadn't heard for years called, 'Something's gotten into my heart'.

'I'd like a drink,' I beckoned to the receptionist. 'Let's be honest – I need a drink.'

'Bar's not open.' She didn't even look up. 'Five-thirty.' She pronounced the words very slowly, as she would to a foreigner. So I sat in the sweaty leather armchair, waiting for my breathing to slow and my hands to stay still. Outside, through the long net curtains, I could see the police stopping all the people who hadn't been involved.

I could have done with a drink. Whisky. Three or four of those. And they'd be only the beginning. But I never got that far. It's funny the way your mind suddenly stops and replays its tapes. I could see the terminal so clearly in the seconds before the attack. The little nun had been talking to me, and then I had reached for the handle on the taxi's door . . .

The nun. The scrubbed features, the inner strength and the deep Irish cadences. When I'd got up from the road, she hadn't been there. I knew that. I could have sworn that. She'd stood right beside me – and then it was as if she had simply disappeared.

For some reason I shivered, sitting on that green leather chair, in the airless, colourless lobby.

In the few seconds it had taken to get my senses moving again, the nun had gone. She had to have gone fast, with her black tresses, and her understanding eyes and those spectacles . . .

Expensive spectacles, for a nun. Gold rims. The chink of vanity. And in that moment I could see how she could have pulled the automatic from her habit, jarred suddenly by a passer-by, jolted out of position, for otherwise she would never have missed. And then turning, even before the shock-wave would have hit those around her, running to the terminal, and then crouching, maybe in a corner, until the trouble had passed.

Perhaps the police had even helped her up. 'Are

you all right, sister, is there anything we can do for you? What a terrible business!' And the smile of forgiveness would have dawned over her flat features, and she would have shone with love and goodwill . . . Did I dream it?

I wished I had. If the KGB were calling on the services of an Irish assassin, it was a lousy sign. They would have picked someone at short notice from their little pool of killers in Berlin – different nationalities that could lose themselves in any country in the world. Such people were kept for the real emergencies. So now there could be no doubt of their intention to shorten my normal lifespan and no sign that they were bothering to ask questions first. The tidying up was gathering momentum.

'Have you got a phone?' I asked the receptionist.

'I thought you wanted a drink . . .'

'I still need a phone.'

'I was going to open the bar specially for you.' She finally looked up. 'Over there, behind the lifts.'

I'm still not sure what made me call old Clarky. Directory Enquiries had his number off pat. And that seemed a good omen. For if I'd had a friend once, maybe I still had him, that day of confusion and violence, when I returned to London.

# THIRTEEN

Alfred Jacob Clark had been a good boy – good enough to win a scholarship from grammar school in London's East End, to the private, boarding school where I eventually met him.

There he'd become known as 'Clarky' – not Alf, not even Jake, especially not Jake – the name for which he so often used to chide his parents.

His father had left Poland in 1938, with a very different name, and had quickly learned the language, the chat and the ways of the British. So winning were *his* ways, that he found himself, at war's end, in an advertising business in London's West End, fully aware that 'there was dosh to make' from the new world rising around him.

In fact Clark senior began to believe, what so many East European *émigrés* end up believing, that there is no limit to the riches of the West, no limit to what they can take.

To prove it, he took himself the wife of the firm's Managing Director, who had, by this time, grown sick of her husband's war stories, not to mention his snoring and his striped pyjamas, through which he seldom offered her the wifely comforts she had enjoyed in earlier years – and, to be truthful, during his absences as well.

Mr Clark, by contrast, lavished on her first his attentions, then his affections, and finally a home in the wilds of Ilford, east of London. Not a great home – for it left so many things to be desired, such as an inside lavatory, plumbing and non-lethal electrics.

Nevertheless the couple were overjoyed. She – plump and jubilant – like a prize cow. He – energetic and rampant, known to the neighbours by the commendably simple and explicit title – the bull. Friends said there wasn't a striped pyjama in the house.

Of course, they were required to pay a price. Clark was forced to leave the advertising firm and set up on his own. And yet, against all odds, the English sun seemed to shine warmly down on his endeavours – all his endeavours. Clarky was born in 1948 in the middle of a smog.

From an early age, the boy knew he would have to escape the parental home. Not that he was deprived of love and comfort. On the contrary, they threatened to overwhelm him.

In fact the house in Ilford, now gaudily re-vamped and re-painted, was swimming on a sea of love. The years had done nothing to dampen the sexual athletics of Clarky's parents. According to local legend – dinner guests, greeted at seven, would be ushered out promptly at 9.45, together with winking and nodding and cries of, 'Isn't he gorgeous?' and, 'Isn't she gorgeous?' as the front door slammed behind them.

Clarky became aware that he had much to live up to, and just as much to live down.

If it hadn't been for the expensive hardship of boarding school, he might never have known normality. Not that there was much of it in the early academic posturing or the dormitory antics of his friends. But they were, at least, boys together. There was companionship. Clarky belonged to a crowd and led it.

In those days, I suppose I considered him a friend. For he possessed the qualities I wanted for myself. He was tall and bright and good at games. He had what kids now call street-cred. Everyone said so.

It wasn't until his final year that we formed any sort of bond. From time to time we would go on walks together, talking about cars or football, or girls – about whom he appeared strangely diffident. Once he took me back to Ilford for tea with his parents – but neither of us enjoyed it. The family was far too rooted in self-congratulation – and to this day I can recall balancing a cake and a glass of orange juice on my knee as Clarky's parents gazed lovingly into their son's eyes and ignored me completely.

Inevitably he won a scholarship to Oxford – a path I was no longer qualified to follow. He studied French and German. He'd also acquired Polish in one of those effortless transfers of skill from father to son. Clarky didn't have to go out and make a life – it came to him.

I remember writing him a couple of letters. And on a blustery October day I took the train to Oxford, to sit in his chilly, damp room in Balliol, toasting crumpets on paper clips attached to the gas fire. We talked about his work, and about all the societies that you joined in your first year and left in the second. He had developed acute back pain, from a bad fall, playing rugby, and he half-lay on the bed, much older somehow than his twenty years, waiting for me to speak. He asked about London, where I was studying but often there were long silences when we simply stared at the leaves gusting in the quadrangle below. Neither of us had made plans for the future. I, too, was learning French and German. I think we imagined we'd end up as teachers.

I didn't go again to Oxford. In fact ten years were to pass before we met again in circumstances neither of us could have foreseen. We crossed at the intersection of three main corridors on the ground floor of the Service. He saw me first, and I knew in that moment, how much he had changed.

We took coffee together in the canteen, and he told me of the nervous breakdown, that I could see written into his features. A tale of doting parents, of premature success in business, of envious friends in envious little Britain – and all of it had come apart on the day when a man put an envelope in his pocket – as a gift – and the gift had been a white substance called Cocaine.

'But I'm one of the lucky ones,' he had said, smiling down over his plastic cup. 'I got out. Three months in the clinic with each day a little harder to face than the one before. But I got out.'

A colleague from Oxford days had introduced him to Fenton. And Fenton hadn't minded about Clarky's sins. 'We use sinners to catch sinners,' he'd assured him. 'Priests can't catch them. We need people who know how they think. But it depends on the quality of your sin. Is it mortal or venal – transitory or endemic? Will it work for us or against us?'

That was Fenton all right. And Clarky had joined the Service then and there, managing parts of the networks in Germany, sticking his life back together – putting his sins to work.

Fenton had been right to hire him. For I got to know Clarky again, within the Service. It was clear the mind was just as formidable as it had been in the old days, even if the body couldn't always keep up. His speciality – a nose for trouble, warning bells in his head. It was as if he could reach out and touch an operation, feeling both its strength and its weakness. Until, that is, the disaster all those years ago, when they had let him go, pension in hand, with no good wishes from anyone.

And what had become of Clarky since then? Not what I expected, when I put the money in the phone box on that day at London airport – home again, with someone trying to kill me.

# FOURTEEN

Clarky told me later that my phone call had made him want to throw up. It was a reflex born out of shock and anger – and for a few minutes after hearing my voice, he had sat in his room, crying soundlessly, beating his palms on the wall – aware that I was bringing back the years he had tried so hard to forget.

I walked into town from Oxford station, still with my East German holdall, and the few East German clothes that hadn't yet fallen apart. And only then did Berlin seem like a distant jail, where the warders had let us out and run away.

Ancient Oxford with its hubbub of normality, its lecturers and all the lectured – and Martin the traitor back amongst them, running, to find a friend.

I thought again of that October day when I'd gone to see Clarky – the bright boy of the seventies, destined to disappoint his expectations. What would his parents have said to him? What would they have done? And what, in any case, was it to me?

And yet perhaps I really had cared about him, for

when he opened the door of his cottage, just off the High Street, it was hard not to gasp. The pain stood out so clearly in his eyes, as we stared at each other over the doorstep, counting the damages of time.

I saw him bite hard into his lower lip. 'You'd better come in.' He shrugged and added, 'Before I change my mind.'

Clarky turned his back, leading the way inside, only he couldn't walk straight. It was as if something heavy was bearing down on his left shoulder. We passed through a narrow corridor lined with prints and portraits in charcoal. I heard the shuffle of his carpet slippers on lino.

We reached a tiny living room, almost filled by a single sofa and then he turned suddenly towards me, his face against the light, so that I saw him more in silhouette than anything else. 'You have two minutes to say whatever you've come to say. No more – understood? And that's only because we were friends.'

'May I sit down?'

He nodded and in that moment I could sense both his hostility and his hurt.

So what did you think, Martin? First time back in four years, and you're looking for the party? You're a cool one, since after all it's you who is the bad egg, the one that stank and had to be destroyed. Lousy traitor, sold up and sold out – what did you come for? I could hear the words, even if he wasn't going to say them.

'I didn't do it, Clarky. You have to know that.'

Instinctively I was whispering. But his face didn't move. So I wasn't even sure he heard me.

And yet something made me decide to tell him: the details, the generalities. The end and the beginning and the dialogue in between.

And all the time I was speaking, he stood in the middle of the room, like a bare winter tree, his back crooked and causing evident pain. But he wouldn't sit down with me, wouldn't share a table or a sofa, or a cup of tea – not with a traitor. Not Clarky.

Through the window I could see the light fading over the garden fence, taking with it my first day back home.

But, had I really imagined this was going home? Didn't I know that homes don't wait for you when you slam the door and walk away, when you push them from your thoughts and your memory. You can't just roll up and open the garden gate – make a fire and warm yourself by the hearth. For a home that's been abandoned is cold and damp – the animals have taken it over, the insects and the birds – and if you're not very, very careful, they'll never let you back.

When I'd finished, Clarky seemed to be asleep on his feet. His head lolled on his chest and even in the semi-darkness I was sure his eyes were shut.

'D'you want a drink?' I heard him ask. And in that moment it was a different voice. More like the one I remembered, from the boy I had known, the fellow who'd won all the school prizes, and was really going somewhere. So quick in mind and body.

Now, for the first time, some of the chill seemed to have left the room – for Clarky was pulling glasses from the sideboard, setting the whisky bottle on the table, snapping the cork, easing himself down beside me.

'I can't believe you're here,' he handed me a glass and drank breathlessly from his own. A few droplets splashed his chin, but he didn't seem to notice. 'Bloody James Martin, consigned to outer darkness and damnation. One-way ticket. Never to return. If you're back the world really has gone mad.'

I swallowed hard, forcing down the whisky, feeling the hot flush spread outwards over my cheeks.

He looked at me as if remembering better times. 'I was already out of the Service when you went over. You remember that.' Clarky crossed his legs. They'd become stiff and the effort made him grimace. 'But they came looking for me the same day you left. "Martin's gone," they said. "And you know where he is." "No," I told them. But they took me in all the same. Full bloody treatment. Just what I needed.' He sighed and put down the glass.

''Course three days later, there you were like some prize pig at a show, mouthing off on television – Fernsehen der DDR – news for the zoo and all that therein was. Eighteen million animals in their cages, slobbering over dinner, switching on to learn absolutely nothing from you.' He shook his head.

'Anyway, by then, they'd let me go. Fenton even came round to apologize, brought me a bottle of wine, said they'd all been a bit on edge.'

'What did they say after I left?'

Clarky got up and switched on a light. 'Much as you'd expect. You were a snivelling little shit who'd been shopping us left right and centre for years. They threw the book at you, my friend – and when they'd done with the first one, they wrote another and threw that too.'

'How d'you mean?'

'Three months after you'd gone, I got a call. Would I stop in and see them. Well by this time I was down here, started a bookshop, gone respectable. Anyway I went. Administrative matter, I reckoned. Probably gone off with too many paper clips in my pocket. When I got in, the boss himself was there. Keen. Old fire and brimstone. Fenton too. They were smiling stupidly. In fact the whole room smelt of booze. I thought – Someone's died, or else they've just increased the budget. Sit down – they said, have a glass.' Clarky picked up his own, examined the contents and drank them. 'Transpired they'd closed the internal investigation into the loss of the GDR networks. That very day. Fenton was having an orgasm, said they'd submitted the report to Downing Street and it had been accepted. End of story.'

'I don't understand. What was the conclusion? Who did they find?'

Clarky looked down at the carpet and I followed his eyes; and it was a cheap carpet and frayed and had probably never been cleaned.

'They found you, my son,' he whispered, turning with difficulty, like an old dog rolling over in its basket. 'They found you.'

So Clarky read me his gospel. And it had been drinks and back-slapping that day in Keen's office. Martin the Mole was crucified in his absence, blamed for everything from treachery to the evil-smelling lavatories. Case closed.

'And did you go along with all of this?' I'd long since finished my whisky and it was clear I wouldn't be offered another.

'I was out of it – I told you.'

'But you thought I was guilty.'

'It fitted, didn't it? The networks in East Germany go to pieces – OK? There's an investigation – and just before you get gutted, you skip over the Wall. Looked pretty watertight to me. How was I to know they were staging your defection? How could anyone know?'

We sat in silence for a while. The rush-hour traffic came and went, the bicycle bells and all the animated talk. The pubs were open, the High Street cleared. And in that moment perhaps we were doing more thinking than the rest of that learned city . . .

'We'll go out for a walk,' Clarky said. 'Bring your things,' and I could see the way his hands had started to fidget. 'Oh, it's not what you're thinking,' he said suddenly. 'I haven't married the bloody bottle or anything like that – but I like to walk, like to get the fresh air.'

There was even some of that around as we squeezed through the narrow front door, along the High, past All Souls and the Sorbonne restaurant and a half-dozen of the newer feeding troughs that hadn't been there on my last visit.

'Of course you will have worked all this out,' said Clarky, licking his lips, adopting one of those Oxford 'I'm-thinking' poses. 'But if you weren't responsible for that disaster in East Germany – there's a fellow still out there who was. And if your airport welcome means anything – he knows you're here.'

Some things in student life don't change, I gather. Lousy coffee, earnest lectures on Namibia, Karl Marx made simple – and the groups of male vigilantes who roam the streets of university towns looking for compliant women.

We passed a few of them, calling out, voices carrying through the narrow streets. Left then, off the main road towards Christ Church and the river

117

beyond. Somewhere, a chapel bell was ringing – loud and long – breaking the peace of the Thames Valley.

At one point we stopped for a moment, hearing an organ, playing deep within one of the colleges. Clarky was panting, and yet for a moment at least, the music made him smile.

'I love hearing them practise,' he said. 'Didn't really appreciate it when we were at school. Now there's plenty of time. Well, since being pensioned off.'

We walked on. The streetlamps cast dabs of pale yellow light as we passed beneath them. 'Of course,' he added, 'after a year or two they offered me the occasional job. Read this, could you Clarky? Read it and let us know what you think. But it's picking up now. Word is I could even be back inside this year. Rehabilitation. End of the Stalinist era.' He stopped and faced me. 'I don't want to wreck that chance. Not again.'

We must have wandered a while in a circle. Eventually without warning Clarky turned into the entrance of a college, taking us through the main quad, up a stone staircase, past books and paintings and into a lecture hall. A portly young man, carrying a furled umbrella, showed us the near-empty rows of chairs. I glanced quickly around.

'What the hell's going on?'

Clarky seemed not to have heard. His eyes were open and yet he was staring fixedly at the floor.

'Do have a cup of cider, if you'd like one,' said the young man, playing with his umbrella, indicating plastic cups and a bottle.

'Yes, do,' said a sickly looking girl. 'I was going to sing,' she said plaintively, taking refuge behind a piano, 'but I caught a cold. So you'll have to do it for me.'

I nodded.

'It's an evening of Edwardian songs,' whispered Clarky. 'History society, meets once a term.'

The piano registered an excruciating chord. The furled umbrella headed for the podium, song-sheet in hand.

It was a straggly little group. Two student girls sang awkwardly behind cupped hands, an elderly don laughed soundlessly to himself in the corner – and at the back, bolt upright, stood a handful of academic zealots who would always take the world more seriously than it deserved.

When I look back, it was the don that worried me. I suppose in my mind I simply didn't want to recognize him, didn't want to remember who he was, didn't want to turn round and have all those old fears confirmed. If I hadn't been so tired, I'd probably have collapsed at the sight of him. But then my capacity for shock had been more or less exhausted.

He was no longer there when Clarky nudged me in the side and jerked his head towards the door. But he was waiting on the stone steps, in the semi-darkness and we followed his back into a study that was light and warm, with modern water colours on the walls, curtains with flecks of yellow on a white background – a spacious room dotted with table lamps and old chairs.

At right angles to the fireplace was a low, square seating unit – a coffee table, set with backgammon and chess boards ... and then the figure turned and chuckled quietly in my direction. Some trip-wire had triggered his laughter, the way it had always done in the past – and now he seemed to babble like a mountain stream.

I had often wondered how he could derive so much amusement from the world around him. But I've since concluded that it was a kind of armour to shield him from the bitter world he inhabited. Francis Keen. Former (I assumed) Director of the Service, a man never accused of charm or social grace.

'You of all people ...' I breathed, and it was an involuntary remark.

'You too,' he replied, not with any amusement, not in a friendly way, not in any way that made me even remotely glad to see him.

# FIFTEEN

The only reason I'd got associated with Keen was because of my mother. Not that she'd ever been sweet on him – or anything like that – but he was a cousin whom she'd felt obliged to comfort and assist. For unlike most people's parents, Keen's had died just a few days *before* the outbreak of war. They had driven down to the coast on that final, blistering hot weekend in 1939, when no one had really believed it would happen. The cricket matches had gone ahead, the cinemas were packed, and Keen's father and mother had bowled along in their open top Armstrong-Siddeley with laughter in their hearts and the champagne flowing.

Not their fault that an army private, who'd never driven anything larger than a bicycle, lost control of his truck on the A30 near Basingstoke. Not their fault they happened to be passing that same stretch of road at exactly the wrong time. Not their fault they weren't around for the six years of misery and destruction that were to follow.

Keen, whatever the extent of his own sorrow,

went on to have an interesting war. From the little my mother said, he seemed to spend it on permanent assignment in some of the continent's most famous holiday spots – only they weren't any longer.

At least when he turned up on our doorstep in 1945, like a pile of dirty laundry, he was confessing to battle fatigue and begging for a good meal. To my regret, and that of my father, the meal was far too good. Keen moved in with us for six tedious months, highlighted by sanctimonious chatter about something called the 'Cold War', and his vision of the battles to come.

Eventually, my mother got him a room with a friend of hers in Kensington – a widow, who lacked adult conversation, and on whom, I seem to recall, Keen made a powerful impression.

For many years, though, he continued to turn up at our house for Sunday lunch. He would arrive during my favourite radio programme of the week – 'Round the Horne', and would add inane comments of his own, or laugh so loudly we would miss the next joke.

And then I remember him coming on a Thursday. I was just down from university, waiting, as I put it then, for the right job. Keen spent a long time talking to my mother in the sitting room, and when I came down he was devouring a plate of buttered toast and a mug of coffee and looking very pleased with himself.

'I'm just going out,' Mum announced, turning red. 'Francis has something to say to you.'

Looking back on it, I thought the whole thing was a huge joke. Keen offering me some kind of lowly post in Military Intelligence, 'Sort of first rung on the ladder, old chap.' But what was even funnier was the idea that he could have been involved in anything half as sensitive as that. I remember thinking they had to be desperate to hire him – and he had to be pretty desperate to approach me.

And yet, after I'd joined, I felt the Service functioned despite Keen's presence – not because of it. We didn't see a lot of each other. In fact, his Sunday lunchtime visits ceased abruptly. Mum said he'd telephoned to tell her – it was probably a conflict of interests, although she failed to see how a hunk of roast beef could be categorized like that.

But it was better that way. In fact Keen and I only met on the occasional routine briefing, a crossing of paths in the corridors, a nod from me, an embarrassed little giggle from him. Unless you include our final encounter.

The way I remember it – Fenton had done the spadework, telling me to defect to the GDR, telling me to dig and burrow. And Keen had provided the patriotic incentives. Vital for Western security. Need to know more than ever. Balance of power at stake.

It hadn't taken more than an hour, and then I got up to leave.

He wasn't going to wish me luck, or any other human emotion. I was just going under for a few years, chucking away all I'd known. Probably of no consequence in the grand scheme of things, and yet, much as it hurt, I had a favour to ask of him.

'I want you to square this with Mum,' I'd said, my hand already on his doorknob. 'Not immediately, but in a week or two. Otherwise I don't think she'll be able to bear it.'

He didn't answer.

'Look,' I went on, 'I know it's vital the other side believes the story. She should be devastated, she should cry and shout, but don't let her suffer too long. Will you do that for me?'

And he had nodded, and shaken my hand, and shut the door behind me. And it was several years before I knew that he'd lied – and that he'd never told my mum, not even when she was dying, holding out her hands for the smallest crumb of comfort the world could offer.

## SIXTEEN

My first impulse was to walk straight out. But I'd
come too far for that and in any case Clarky had
manoeuvred himself behind me, not in a sinister
way, but the message was clear enough.

And so we stood, the three of us – Keen, no
longer chuckling, but staring at me with evident
curiosity. Such a British little gathering. Awkward,
embarrassed, with plenty of undertones of hostility. And it seemed to me that as a nation we are
poorly equipped for social occasions – even the
lousy ones. We don't have the easy, informal flow
of the Americans, or the rigid, procedural
approach of the Germans – just a lot of fidgeting
and looking elsewhere. Even a handshake seems
excessively familiar.

I sat down without being asked.

'You'll take a drink, won't you?' said Keen.

'No thanks,' I replied. 'I didn't come here
through choice.'

'That's not quite true, is it?' Keen raised a single
eyebrow and sat down opposite. Clarky stayed
where he was beside the door. 'I mean no one

asked you to leave East Berlin, did they?'

'My mission was over – or rather the rug was taken out from under it.'

'Why d'you say that?' Keen looked genuinely puzzled.

'Oh, no reason really. The Wall's come down, Germany's re-unified under Nato, the Soviets are going home.' I shook my head at him. 'It was time to come home and count the daggers in my back – don't you think?'

Clarky moved forward a pace. 'I think you should tell him,' he looked across at Keen, and I wondered whether, after all, he wasn't on my side.

Keen sat back in the chair and farted loudly. He had always belonged to the mannerless section of the upper class.

'I suppose I should,' he said to no one in particular. 'After all it's been a long time. When was it you left, Martin?'

'Four years ago.'

'Quite.' He pulled a dirty handkerchief from his trouser pocket and dabbed at his nose. I remembered he never could leave himself alone – always poking at one orifice or another, or scratching his testicles.

Keen looked at me as an object of only passing interest. 'I'm sorry we had to stick so many daggers in your back, as you put it, but then your back was at least some distance away – and you didn't feel much pain – did you?' He raised a hairless eye-brow. 'Besides, my dear fellow, it was necessary.'

'You'll be telling me next that I served Queen and country . . .'

'You certainly did,' Keen smiled dangerously, 'although not in the way you imagined. All right you went to East Berlin and burrowed into the Stasi, but the fact of your going was more import-ant to us back here. We knew there was a traitor who'd sold out on all the GDR networks, we even narrowed it down to a little group of suspects, but there was no proof. We would have needed a confession, and we weren't going to get it. Sure you won't have a drink?' He got up as if to pour himself one, but changed his mind.

'We were faced with two choices. We could either get rid of all possible candidates – or learn to live with it, keep tracking and investigating and hope they'd eventually make a mistake. So we chose the second option.' He propped his head on his elbow. 'My feeling has always been that treachery is a bit like shoplifting in a big store. You're always going to get someone doing it. Might as well know that right from the start – then you can do something about it. Anyway we blamed it all on you – had a general clear out and let them think they'd got away with it. So everyone would probably have lived peacefully ever after if it hadn't been for you blundering out of East Berlin, looking for answers.'

'It wasn't quite like that.'

'No,' he smiled. 'I don't expect it was.' He took off his glasses and looked at me, unblinkingly. 'I think it's time you and I had a long talk.'

'Why should I trust you?'

'Should is the wrong word,' he replied. 'But you don't appear to have many friends out there.'

'Just you and the Stasi . . . ?'

'There are stranger things. Both of us could have disposed of you by now, if we'd wanted. Talk to me,' he smiled inappropriately, 'while you still can.'

'How much safer will that make me?'

'Tomorrow, Martin. I'm here all tomorrow.'

He wasn't smiling as I made for the door. 'Look,' he added. 'Bit of unfinished business – that thing with your mother. Very sorry about it. But I couldn't tell her. Not if they were to believe your story. There was evidence that the Stasi watched her for a very long time after you'd gone over. Insurance, I suppose.'

I turned and looked at him, and I couldn't help feeling that for all the Sunday meals, and all the companionship and friendship she'd offered over so many years, my mother had deserved something a great deal better, better than him and better than all of us – me included.

If that encounter passed for the grateful thanks of the Nation, for nearly five wasted years of my life –

it wasn't much. Seeing Keen hadn't been much either. I knew I couldn't trust him, but just how bent had he become? In this business it has always been a question of degree.

Clarky seemed disgruntled. 'I'm sorry about all that,' he said, as we emerged into the quadrangle. It was raining. Somewhere in the distance a siren was blaring. 'But I had to tell him you were coming. Rules.'

'He's bloody complacent these days.'

'He can afford to be. Oxford don – all the facts on Goethe and Schiller and a bit of Brecht thrown in for the real trendies.'

The sirens were getting louder, three or four of them, by the sound of it.

'Anyway,' said Clarky, 'come back to my place and we'll work something out.'

God knows I needed a place to go. The encounter with Keen demanded some pretty close scrutiny. Men like that had long ago turned lying into an art form.

We had reached the High Street and even at that distance it wasn't hard to tell something was wrong. There was a small crowd gathering at the head of Magpie Lane. Police cars had halted traffic, and an officer with chequered tape was sealing the entrances. No sirens now. Maybe they'd been ambulances or fire engines – probably in position by then.

And I don't know why I hadn't seen it earlier, the

black smoke rising above the houses, driven hard by the wind, scurrying away into the night.

Clarky had hobbled ahead of me, and both of us were running down the High, past the pubs, ignoring the traffic. An ambulance emerged, lights flashing at the corner, not stopping for the police to remove their cordon, bursting straight through the chequered tape. And we were at the corner now – Clarky straining his head, looking up the narrow alley.

'Gas main,' someone was saying.

He turned back to me and even in the darkness, with all the strange flashing lights, I could see he'd changed colour.

'Get out of here,' he whispered. 'Now.'

We pushed our way through the people, some of them giggling, others with drinks in their hands, emerging from the pubs in search of amusement.

Clarky didn't stop until we reached the Randolph Hotel, but he wouldn't go in. We could see people having dinner in the window, a world away.

I caught my breath. 'Clarky, what is it?'

'The house is gone.' He licked dry lips and I could see his hands were shaking. 'An explosion. Looked as though the whole thing disintegrated. It was only paper thin. Old place . . .'

'But what . . . ?'

'Don't talk, don't say anything. Just keep up with me. We're leaving.'

'But there's everything you had in there.'

'There was nothing,' he replied quickly. 'Nothing at all – just books. And now they've blown those up.'

He started walking fast. 'Move, I said. Quickly.'

'Clarky, what about Keen? Maybe we should see . . .'

'Leave him.'

Clarky had a car, parked across town. Something grey, with four doors, and it didn't smell and it didn't make much noise – and so, after all the years in East Germany, it certainly got my vote.

I must have fallen asleep for I remember nothing until the lights of a motorway café.

He bought me coffee, under the bright neon beams, and I watched an elderly couple holding hands across a table, young men with bleached blond hair – people of the night, pale and tired like us. A waitress in uniformed trilby cleared the dishes, picking her way among the plants, that looked as though they, too, could have done with a meal. Fast food, there was, available to animals and vegetables alike. 'Pot of tea and your choice of cake' a sign was offering pensioners . . . and as my eyes wandered so did my mind.

In that moment the exhaustion struck me – day one, the day I left Berlin and came West.

I looked across the table. Clarky held his head in his hands. As for me, I counted myself lucky I still had mine.

# SEVENTEEN

In the dawn landscape almost any city can look like East Berlin – lifeless, deficient, the kind of place to drive past and never stop in – if only you could.

She had to have been an old girlfriend of Clarky's – the woman in Penfold Street, near to the Westway, standing there with her lips moist and her dressing-gown peeping open and an expression that seemed to recall the lust of days long past.

It was shortly after sunrise and we had tipped up on her doorstep, and she wasn't surprised – only mildly amused.

'Hallo, Doll,' she said to Clarky and I could see that she wouldn't have been bad looking back then, wasn't bad looking even now, with the sleep still in her eyes, and the pillow lines etched out on her cheek.

We went inside and Clarky said, 'He's tired,' pointing at me. 'Have you got somewhere for him to sleep?'

I wasn't just tired, I was finished, no longer concerned whether the city outside was London or East Berlin, or whether someone was making a lousy job of trying to kill me. So I slept from that early morning through to the next, barely stirring, unaware of the relentless rain.

Clarky said he'd been glad I was out of the way. A good opportunity to re-travel the lanes with Iris in her dressing-gown – If you can call having your house blown up and coping with me 'an opportunity'.

They were heavily into the session when I got out of bed. I could hear them in the next room, squelching their way through the bodily rituals, as the traffic blared at eye level into the city. It reminded me of the carnal diversions of East Berlin, first provided through State channels, then later obtained by my own laborious efforts.

Kirsch, ever the organizer, had come round to see me after I got back from Moscow, and like a travelling salesman had produced a photo-album from his briefcase. 'Choose yourself a Christmas present, Herr Martin,' he had said, pointing at black and white pictures of women in their underwear. 'A bit of warmth. After all it's been a long time, *nicht wahr*?'

In fact the little shit knew exactly how long it had been. At the office they'd probably had a good laugh about it. Martin hasn't had a fuck for a year, they'd have said. Poor devil.

And those days maybe I was desperate, for I did do a little shopping from Kirsch's catalogue. Mostly they had been functional episodes, at times

133

comforting, even amusing, and yet frequently I had been left with a feeling of overwhelming loneliness and frustration.

That morning I sat at the kitchen table in Penfold Street, watching the rain-spattered cars, aware as I had been for the last four years, that all roads led back to Cassie. And maybe it was pure co-incidence, or part of a grand design, that led my old schoolfriend to get out of bed at that same moment and come into the kitchen, offering to tell me what had really happened to her and where she was.

I remember so clearly the tightening in my stomach, as he started to speak – the same feelings I'd had whenever I saw her – back in the old days in London. She would emerge from a crowd or open a door, and it was as if a hand were reaching inside me, jolting my heart.

Somehow our minds would lock together, giving a sense of extraordinary purpose – undiminished by time or distance. Cassie didn't dominate my life – she simply joined it. Along the dismal streets of Moscow and East Berlin her vision lit me a brighter path.

Clarky may have read some of this in my eyes, for he started a sentence and then changed tack – and his tone seemed kinder, as if he realized I would take it all badly.

'You didn't know any of this, did you?' he asked.

'I mean there wasn't really anyone you could approach . . .'

I nodded.

'Look old friend . . .' he took in my empty cup, 'more tea?'

'Clarky, why don't you . . . ?'

'OK, OK, this is it.' He stopped fiddling with the teapot and put it down. 'About a month after you disappeared, she returned to America, went to Langley, they said. Something in intelligence assessment. I was out by then, but one of the other old crocks told me. Fellow from archives.'

Keep going Clarky, I thought. Spit it all out, however nasty it tastes.

'Anyway for about a year no one heard anything of her. Fenton got posted to Washington to try to mend fences. The special relationship wasn't looking so special at that point. Anyway they had new priorities – we had new priorities . . . you know what it was like.' He poured himself some tea, as if suddenly lacking the strength to continue. 'Well, she must have run into Fenton out there . . .'

'Why don't you call her Cassie? After all it's her name . . .'

'Sorry,' he looked away. 'Cassie ran into Fenton, 'course she did. You know one of those bloody liaison things. But anyway it went further than that. The next I heard was that she'd got engaged to him. They were married shortly after . . .' he paused.

I think maybe my mouth had fallen open.

'Fenton married Cassie,' he said.

And still I couldn't speak, sitting in that dull, cheap little flat near the Westway, as the rest of the world woke up, shouted outside the window, laughed, chattered, turned on their radios, ran their showers and went off to work. And I died just a little, deep down and way out of sight.

We were glad of the tea. After half an hour Iris came in and sat down, still in her dressing-gown.

'You want something stronger?' She looked at both of us in turn. And I think that if I'd said, 'Yes', Clarky would have done the same.

Eventually I cleared my throat. 'What else is there, Clarky? Fill it in for God's sake. You must know more than that.' And to jog his mind I told him how Cassie had arrived on Fenton's doorstep the morning after my car accident on the Edgware Road. So, maybe there'd been something going on even then. But he shook his head.

'Nothing to back that up, my friend. Nothing at all.'

'But it's pretty odd, isn't it?'

'It's all odd,' Clarky snorted. 'Ever met anyone in this game who was normal? Look at them. The whole lot would have been a credit to the local lunatic asylum.' He shook his head. 'You have to be joking, they never went for anyone who was normal.'

'Cassie was normal.'

136

Clarky made a face. 'Of course she wasn't. If she had been, you wouldn't have gone so bloody crazy about her. She was always special. We all knew that, long before you tipped your hat at her. She had personality, she was fun, she had outside interests.' He pointed a finger at me. 'She didn't fit, my friend. I'm not saying anything else, not casting aspersions, but she didn't fit.'

Later, of course, Clarky and Iris went back to bed to 'think things through', and I even managed a laugh at that, as I wandered out into the afternoon rain.

I'd forgotten how utterly depressing and dirty London can seem. Forgotten because when I'd last been there, I'd seen it through Cassie's eyes, and she had always been very American and very enthralled.

The drizzle reminded me of the only cliché she and I had ever shared – the weekend in Brighton, the boarding house by the sea, the nosy landlady and the damp sheets, the nudges and winks in the dining room, and the eyes that roamed down to our ring fingers, looking for clues.

It was all there, just as the brochures said it would be.

We hadn't quite signed in as Mr and Mrs Smith, because government employees with our kind of pedigree don't do that sort of thing. We had both made phone calls, saying where we were, only she had been obliged to say who she was with. Americans are that much more curious.

'It's all right,' she had smiled. 'They don't mind me being with you. You're Nato.'

'Hallo, I'm Nato.'

She had thrown a pillow across at me.

'They simply want to make sure I'm not shacking up with a Bulgarian diplomat and telling him what we get in the canteen on Thursdays . . .'

'It would have come out in your annual lie detector test.'

She grinned. 'It always does.'

I threw the pillow back. 'Why does the CIA hire you?'

'Fear,' she laughed again. 'Fear at the damage I'd cause if I was let out into the real world.'

Everything had been in place that weekend – the sea along the beach, the rain along the front, the old people crouching in their beach shelters, staring into the wind that stabbed at the coastline and sent another summer to hell. Most were alone, and we watched for a while from our window, as one by one they got up and shuffled beneath us, with their sticks and their plastic hair covers, while the weather beat so unjustly down on them.

'I don't want to get old,' Cassie had whispered.

'You won't.'

'No I mean it,' she turned to me. 'I don't want to feel that it's all running out – the time, the energy. I don't want to regret anything.'

'And do you?'

'I can't tell how I'll feel in the future.'

'Leave the future to me.'

'That's the danger.' And she put her head on my chest, once again the child, needing reassurance.

Later when we lay together, she kissed me hard on my face and forehead. 'I love the person you are,' she said.

'Which means?'

'Which means that if you have to ask, you aren't that person.'

So many layers there were to Cassie. Many she showed. Many she kept in the shadows. And there I never tried to venture, afraid that I would find no place for myself, afraid to steal her secrets, afraid she would never forgive me if I did.

And now I was walking back to the flat, knowing that I had to see her, feeling the need building inside me, pushing away the years of absence and emptiness.

I must have been desperate.

How else, I wondered later, could I have crept into the flat, checked on the closed bedroom door, found Clarky's wallet and credit cards, a cheque book, a wad of money from Iris's handbag – and taken them all?

'Sorry, but I had to do this,' I wrote in her lipstick on the back of a newspaper bill. 'I'll pay you back, soon as I can.'

And I took my holdall and flagged a taxi to the

airport, and no longer noticed where I was going or who was around me.

Everywhere I looked I saw Cassie's face and for hours on end there was sunshine around it and the clear blue sky out over the Atlantic. It seemed for the first time in so many years that I had left the clouds behind.

## EIGHTEEN

From East Berlin to Washington.

Even saying that to myself made me laugh hysterically.

For it must surely be ridiculous to transfer simply by means of an aircraft from the dead to the living. First thought as I unloaded my East German holdall from the taxi and carried it into the hotel.

And you know the way people tell you, 'This isn't just any hotel.' Well, this was. I'd asked the taxi to take me downtown, and only when we'd passed two or three places did I pick one – all chrome and leather, the way they'd begun to build them in East Berlin for the foreigners.

It wasn't my first visit to Washington. But once you've lived in the GDR everywhere feels like a first visit. I found myself walking out, simply gazing in shop windows, staring at pullovers and trousers and shoes as if I'd just swung down from a tree.

I had always liked America. Not for the good or the bad, but because it contained both in such startling and immense quantities. The land of limousines and beggars, the best in the world and the worst in the world – only they never seemed to know the difference. Just turn on the television, I recalled, and good taste was rammed down your throat with the same gusto as bad taste. The talented got equal airtime to the morons.

That was a classless society, if any of those East Germans could have realized it. One of the US presidents had got it right ... something about growing up poor in America, where the beauty was not to realize it.

Even I wasn't poor. Not with Clarky's funds. Poor Clarky.

I found M Street on the grid, remembering that it eventually bumps its way into Georgetown. There, it seemed, you could die of overeating within minutes. And yet, peering into the windows, I couldn't help feeling some of the old East German suspicions crowding back in. What if it were all gone tomorrow? Shouldn't I go shopping while I had the chance? How much would I have to bribe the shopkeepers to get what I really wanted – assuming I could ever identify it?

It was a world outside and beyond and totally disconnected from the one I'd left. The easy affluence, the easy manners. The ideology was unwritten and unimposed. All that was required of you was to survive.

I sat in a café and wondered if I would. The KGB wanted to 'tidy me up' before I could discover the identity of their agent in Britain. Keen seemed content to watch while they did it, hoping he'd learn something. And I had, somehow, to go back through each of my former contacts, hoping to worry one of them into the open. What then?

'A medal, I think for Martin, don't you?' In my mind I could hear Keen's voice talking to someone. 'Pity it's got to be posthumous, but we can't just chuck them around. Everybody'd want one.'

I must have eaten a lot. A beef sandwich arrived – more like a cow strapped between two slices of bread. Some apple pie – the way my mother had never made it – beer and coffee, and my stomach was hinting strongly at revolt as I lurched back down the street.

A party of young girls giggled on their way past – and in that moment I was surrounded by the light-bright drawl, the loose language and the T-shirt climate. Land of Cassie. And for the first time in so many years I could feel her close. Not a comfortable, not an easy sensation – a little like the fear of an impending storm. Man standing powerless in nature's path.

And I was weak. I can say that now. Four years of making do had sapped my will and my resolve. I had lived on substitute rations. Sex for love. Lies for truth. The past for the future. And so when I returned to the hotel I caught the glance thrown at me across the lobby and sent it back.

The girl was hardly beautiful, with her short blond hair and tomboy walk and quick, efficient movements. Perhaps it was my East German conditioning – if people offer, you take. So we went up together in the lift and my hand shook a little as I unlocked the door. The room was colder than it had been earlier, or perhaps she was already siphoning off some of the warmth – her left hand snaking to the zip behind her back, and everything falling away from the tanned little body in one so practised gesture.

Maybe I had thought that for ten minutes or twenty or however long the dollars lasted, she could somehow fill the gap that Cassie had left me.

But as she pulled back the covers we both seemed to realize it wouldn't work. She smiled and shrugged, crossing the thin, brown legs, reaching for a cigarette. She started to speak, 'Some days,' she said, and then stopped and smiled again. 'Look, mister . . . you don't really need this, and for some reason I don't need it either. Money's fine, but maybe we're just tired.'

I nodded.

'Where are you from?' she asked, and that threw me, because you can't go round America saying you're from East Germany. They burn people at the stake for that, don't they? Like saying you're from Venus, or a lunatic. And God, if you'd lived there for any length of time you'd see they had a point. Eighteen million people choosing to live behind a wall simply because the government built one. Now there's complacency for you. There's a yellow, craven little streak, and not just in the flag either.

'I said where are you from?' She finished the cigarette and got up as if she were already dressed.

'Nowhere you've heard of.'

'Try me.'

'I almost did.'

She laughed then, and she had a wide mouth, full of those chiselled American teeth, which always made kissing American mouths so different.

'I haven't paid anything . . .'

'That's OK. I didn't do anything. And you can have the look for free.'

She was dressed as suddenly as she'd been naked, and it was only to me that it made any difference. She leant against the door, visibly without cares.

'Anyway, I'm glad I tried you,' she said.

'Why?'

'Because you looked a nice man.'

'Thanks.'

'And . . .'

'And what?'

'Because a man called Kirsch told me to do it. And I *was* paid.'

She was looking straight at me now, but it wasn't a sinister gaze. She didn't know the importance of what she was saying, didn't know that she'd sliced me into my component parts, more certainly and more shockingly than any surgeon.

'He said Kirsch meant "cherry" in German,' she went on. 'So maybe that kind of fits the job!'

Strange as it sounds I slept well that night, perversely glad that Kirsch was in town and playing the old routines. They'd amuse him, lighten him up, ready for the time when he'd have to go to the scrapyard.

I knew then that whatever happened with the traitor, I'd get rid of Kirsch myself, once he'd outlived his usefulness.

I was reminded of the old Polish joke from the eighties, when they thought the Warsaw Pact were going to invade. 'Who would you kill first,' one man asks his friend, 'Russians or East Germans?'

'East Germans,' came the reply. 'Business before pleasure.'

Kirsch was business.

## NINETEEN

I didn't know it then. For Clarky's version of events didn't come out until much later. But by this time he'd already left London for Berlin.

Together with Iris he went to ground, the way he'd been taught, the way he'd done it in the early eighties, the way we'd all done it – only to discover the ground had moved.

'We drove straight for Checkpoint Charlie,' she told me later, 'missed the bloody turning and found ourselves in the middle of East Berlin. I could have died. Clarky's hands were really shaking.'

Course they were, Clarky. Course they were.

Now at least he knew something of the nausea that had gripped *my* insides for the last four years. No pregnant woman had ever suffered morning sickness more intensely than me, looking out each day at the eastern zone, thinking about the grey, stupid, little men who'd built it. Sick to the core, I'd felt. Sad too.

After that, Clarky said, he'd played it by the book. Made the calls, done the rounds.

He'd bought a yellow Beetle and started with

Christian because Christian had been one of the Service favourites. A big fellow in many senses – the nose, the jaw, the hands that wandered over women, with the same drive and enthusiasm as the ancient explorers had wandered over Africa.

Christian ran a second-hand car shop near Spandau where he'd done the business for anyone who paid. For years he'd sculpted his own deals across the Wall, getting fancy cars for the élite, getting them serviced, buying and selling his way into the graces of East Germany.

It was Capitalism, handmade for Communists – expensive and highly select. A Party official had a favourite daughter who yearned for a Porsche, a Mercedes was needed as a bribe, an old general wanted an Alfa Romeo while he could still get his arthritic legs into it. And Christian had been the provider – discreet, apolitical, the perfect fellow without a history.

But in 1983 he graduated. After weeks of secret negotiations he delivered a Jaguar to the wife of the East German Interior Minister – equipped with extras that she hadn't even dreamed of ordering. Among them, a short-range, low-powered transmitter that not only gave away the vehicle's position, but also picked up any conversations inside it.

Armed with the correct frequencies he made his way to the offices of the British Military government beside the Olympic Stadium and asked for the commanding officer. An odd, almost burlesque figure, standing in dirty jeans, cocky and irreverent in the dark, little reception, adorned with regimental flags and plaques and traditions he'd never heard about.

Christian received the standard welcome – condescension, a polite smile of disbelief and a mug of coffee. Four hours later, though, after dinner in the Officers' mess, a bottle of claret, much handshaking and toasts, very few of them sincere, he was chauffeured home, helped up the stairs to his apartment and wished a 'good-night' that he was too drunk to hear. While he slept a man watched his door. He didn't know it then, but he was on the payroll.

Ironically, I was the first desk officer to view the fruits of Christian's operation. The same night that he'd given us the radio frequencies of the Jaguar, we had tuned in to discover its lady owner in deep breathing exercises, while parked close to the lake at Potsdam. Although unaccompanied by her husband, she nonetheless felt free to discuss his business, his colleagues and his shortcomings at home. So within a few hours we had the most detailed, intimate picture ever, of the household of East Germany's Interior Minister. In our terms, therefore, and on day one, Christian was pure gold.

I had assumed he would have left Berlin once the Wall came down. After all the Service had paid him enough – he could have gone almost anywhere in the world and sold almost anything. But some-how, even though the war had ended, he couldn't leave the field of battle. Clarky found him, still in Spandau, with a larger showroom, more bunting, and much bigger discounts on offer. And, accord-ing to Iris it was strange how 'German' the man had become. A lot of talk about, 'Now we are one people again, *ja*?' and, 'It was good finally to see families united and happy again . . .' and so Clarky would have known he was lying. That wasn't so surprising. Christian had no idea what Clarky was up to – and you could never just barge your way into Berlin without people checking you over – and over again, and still trying to push your face in the river.

An exciting city – if you didn't mind dying.

They had talked in the office, beneath the girlie trade calendars from all the years gone by, and Christian hadn't said much. Business was OK, life was OK, the wife wasn't OK – but then she never really had been – and what about dinner?

He suggested the Ganymede.

'But that's in the East,' Clarky had retorted.

'And now we are all one happy city.' Christian smiled and winked and said he'd see him at eight.

'I have someone with me,' said Clarky, '. . . er, a woman.'

'Then I shall have a woman too,' replied Christian, as if to show that whatever Clarky could manage, he could too.

*   *   *

Clarky and Iris arrived early. Christian and friend were late. 'A thousand forgivenesses,' he declared, his English momentarily deserting him, as he swept into the restaurant and kissed Iris on both cheeks. 'Allow me to introduce Heidi.'

Heidi's leather-clad bottom slid audibly over the cushions and came to rest next to Clarky. He smiled limply at her, taking in the shiny face, and the aggressive teeth. Heidi was dressed and made up to be forty, even though she no longer was. But that was her sticking point. The hair and the clothes said so.

'Zo,' she sighed, and thereafter left the conversation to Christian.

The Ganymede's food had improved with time. Iris ordered pepper steak, Heidi had duck and so did Christian. Clarky didn't seem to remember what he ate.

Christian talked incessantly about the new BAY EM VAYS, as he called them. 'BMWs', Clarky whispered to Iris.

'But really,' Christian complained, 'it is all they want – these people from the East. You suggest they might like a Fiat or a Peugeot, but they turn down their noses at this. A little old lady comes into my showroom. The Wall has been down for just a week. God knows why but the banks have offered her a loan for a car. What does she want? A BAY EM VAY. Nothing else will do the trick. I ask

151

why. She says it's German and that's all that matters.' He looked admiringly across the table to Heidi. 'I also like things that are German,' he grinned. 'They are beautifully engineered.' She grinned back. 'But they don't always have much character,' he added, and licked his lips noisily. Instantly, Heidi's face coloured and the smile left her. She gulped and looked down at the table-cloth.

It was an awkward and cruel thing to say – and it seemed to puncture the little dinner party. Iris tried to make small talk with Heidi, Clarky and Christian chatted vaguely about the future. Waiters came and went through long dark curtains. They bowed and whispered and pretended not to listen to the conversation.

Only after coffee did Christian lean back in his chair to signal that the social chit-chat, such as it was, had finished.

'How are you enjoying the Hotel Castor?' he asked suddenly.

Clarky didn't move. 'I don't believe I told you where we were staying . . .'

'Room 305,' continued Christian, 'the double bed, not the twin. You arrived the day before yesterday on PanAm 1065 from Frankfurt. You,' he looked hard at Iris, 'you live at 24 Penfold Street, London, West two.' He stopped abruptly as if waiting for applause. 'I could go on . . .'

'Please yourself,' said Clarky. 'It's late. We have

to be going. Thanks for dinner.' He pushed his chair away from the table.

Christian rose and put a hand on his shoulder.

'My friend, you would after all, expect me to check.'

Clarky sat down again. 'Check what?'

'What you are doing. Look my friend. Four years ago the Service shuts the big door in your face. OK? Finish. All right,' he waved a hand in the air, 'once we were friends. We ran around together, got frightened, saved a few lives, lost a few . . . and now you come back wanting what? Dinner? A new car?'

It was Clarky's turn to smile. For in that moment there could be no doubt Christian was as good as he'd ever been. Christian had checked and done his homework. Christian was plugged in and operating. It was the best news Clarky could have asked for. Even with the Wall down, Berlin still had a network, and now he had made contact.

Heidi took care of Iris, which was presumably the reason she'd been there.

And in a light drizzle Christian led Clarky out to his car, holding open the passenger door and ushering him inside. 'This is a Renault my friend – much more comfortable than a BAY EM VAY – but to get people here to try it. Uh!'

It was dark and late and Berlin had long since gone indoors as the Renault glided over wet cobbles. Hard for Clarky to get his bearings. So long since he'd travelled the eastern sector and there never had been time to get your bearings. Rush jobs, all of them, with your heart in your bloody throat, and your last good meal swilling about in your stomach in case you didn't get another. Oh, Berlin had often been the trip to end them all.

'We go to meet some old friends, discuss what is best to be done. And then you can tell us what you want – OK?'

Clarky nodded in the darkness at the tramlined streets.

And then they had pulled up and Christian was out of the car in a hurry, Clarky limping behind. Into a courtyard now, up two or three steps and they were inside an apartment block, a stone corridor, tiny lamps set crookedly into the walls.

He followed Christian into an apartment which already seemed full of people. Clarky glimpsed a crowded kitchen, a kettle on the stove, more faces in the hall and the living room, and someone cleared a place for him in front of the television.

A middle-aged man in a black leather jacket told one or two figures to leave, and shut the door behind them. Clarky counted four who remained – two men, two women, there wasn't time to take in their faces. But he didn't like it, any of it. Somehow it felt too exposed.

Christian did the introductions. There was a

Hans and a Barbara and a Lisa but it didn't mean anything.

'I'm sorry,' Clarky shook his head, and all his gloomy presentiments seemed to have been justified. 'I think we should talk somewhere more private. I don't know who your colleagues are and with all due respect . . .' He made for the door, but the man in the leather jacket blocked him.

Christian put out a hand to his shoulder. 'I'm sorry too,' he said. 'But for the moment you should stay here.' He grimaced and opened his palms in a gesture of resignation. 'You do not have much choice, my friend. Berlin is not the same city it was. There are new rules. You do business here, or not at all.'

Clarky sat perfectly still, trying to weigh up all the options he'd just thrown away.

# TWENTY

Me?

I didn't want that day to begin, any more than Clarky. For so long I had crammed my mind with all sorts of daydreams and visions and strange imaginings. How would it really be, seeing Cassie? What would I feel? Could the day – this day – come when I would turn a corner or open a door and find her?

I realize now that dreams are easy to live with. They don't change, they don't argue. They're new and bright whenever you want them. And maybe I had grown used to her as a dream – perhaps the real person was someone I had never known, someone who had, in any case, forgotten me long ago.

So, I put off the moment, leaving the hotel in the early morning sunshine, seeing the smoke curling off the sidewalks from the ventilators and car parks underground. Of course, I argued, the two of us could talk for a moment – and then I might go away and in all probability we'd never see each other again – so what would I lose?

But I knew the answer to that. I needed something from Cassie — not a commitment, not an answer, but something that would fill the void she had created.

And there was another side. Together we had to think our way back to those days in London, retrace the events, recreate what might have happened.

I hired a car and motored slowly through Georgetown towards the suburbs of Chevy Chase. There, the past seemed so irrelevant among the neat white colonial houses, the newly coiffed gardens and lawns. America came to the world without the baggage and the dead-weight of history. It was free to look forward — not back.

Of course they had known little of the Cold War. To them it had been taken care of by a few dozen missile silos stretched out in chains across the south central states. As long as they functioned, the country slept calmly and went on making money. No one got their feet wet crossing the inner German border with three Alsatians snapping behind and a minefield out in front.

Whichever way you looked at it, we in Europe had been alarmingly close to the action. And if you'd worked a few years in the Stasi, then you knew how close it had really got.

I had found Fenton's address in the Washington Directory — Mr and Mrs Fenton, more precisely — Brandywine Street NW — such a charming little address, you'd have thought. And the moment I saw the houses I could picture all the diplomatic functions they hosted there – the dinners, the cocktail parties, the fine dresses and the guests who would leave early to attend the White House in the morning. Smart and very powerful this Brandy-wine Street. I could see it all – but I couldn't see Cassie there. Not the Cassie with all the fun in her eyes and the laughter. She could play the game, same as the rest of us. But to make a life of it?

I parked about forty yards down the street. The house had a wide double door and two pillars, and a lawn, sprayed lazily by automatic jets. Two women in tennis clothes came down the path and got into a convertible sports car. It was peaceful and well-ordered – and no place for me or the baggage I carried.

I didn't know if Cassie was there. Clarky had said she still worked at Langley. So maybe she had left for the day. It was already mid-morning and north-west Washington would be dressing itself for the shopping malls and the aerobics classes, and maybe a playgroup or two for the mothers. And which are you now, Cassie? Which are you?

A station wagon was parked in the drive. Inside the house there would be a cleaner, perhaps a cook as well. Even now they might be discussing the dinner party for that evening.

'Go away, Martin, leave her alone,' said a voice inside me. 'She's better off without you. She's made a life. What the hell can you give her?'

I wiped a hand across my forehead. It came away wet and cold. And then I could see the front door open and a short woman in black emerged. She carried a sweeping brush and began beating the flagstones and tidying the flower pots. She was young and suntanned, perhaps from Central America or the Philippines. And she'd be willing and servile, and Cassie wouldn't like it at all. Not being waited on, not living in all this cushioned splendour. As I watched I recalled the way we'd always said we'd live – a flat in the city centre – any city, any flat. But it would be small and simple and near the restaurants – and we'd eat out and travel and . . .

The woman finished her work and went indoors. And you do it now, I told myself, or you go to the airport, forget about her and never come back.

It was simple, really, the way complex matters often are. There was this figure in his nylon shirtsleeves and ill-fitting green trousers, made in East Germany, and he gets out of his car, and walks up the street, so awkward as to be laughable, and he takes the front path, trying to shake off the weight of a thousand memories, crowding in and making him dizzy – and that was me.

Inside the porch I leaned against the wall for a moment, just to steady myself before ringing the bell, speech prepared, mouth firmly shut in case it fell open.

'I've come to see Mrs Fenton,' I said, looking down, because the maid was shorter than me, speaking precisely in case she couldn't quite grasp my English. Only it wasn't the maid. Instead, a set of dark eyes and a smile that seemed to rush at me from my past – and maybe there was a second or two of silence, but her arms were pulling me towards her and I could feel her face and her hair next to me. Quite suddenly something was making me shudder and fight for breath, and my heart seemed to be beating itself to destruction.

For several minutes we stood holding each other in the cool of the hallway. Someone passed us without speaking. A telephone rang distantly in another part of the house, but we were crossing back through time and nothing could disturb us.

In the end Cassie led me to a window seat that looked out on to a garden of quiet and shade. We didn't talk. Eventually she fetched me a glass of water, and when I reached for it my hand started to shake, quite out of control.

'Martin, are you a sentimental sort of fellow?'

'No, sir.'

'Not at all?'

'Well, how d'you mean, sir?'

'I mean – do you get silly over girls, do you long for their company, do you get lonely and moody and . . . ?'

'Does it cloud my judgement?'

'Precisely.'

'No, it doesn't.'

'I see.'

He hadn't really seen at all, the Service's medical officer, giving me the standard mental assessment, all those years ago.

Funny how you think back to those things – because if the stupid bugger had seen me in that grand house on Brandywine Street, mooning over Cassie and wanting to cry my eyes out, he'd probably have failed me then and there.

Best not to think of it.

Gradually, I unclamped my hands from her. The face was paler than I remembered, the hair swept further from it, behind her ears, the freckles in isolated bunches around the nose and eyes.

She was going to speak but the words wouldn't come.

'Cassie, we'll talk,' I said. 'Not now maybe. Bit of a shock this. I'm so sorry, but I couldn't really telephone.'

'I know.' She tried to smile.

And why was it I wanted to go? I suppose I couldn't bear to hear that she was busy, or had friends coming round, or was going away to a life that had nothing whatever to do with me.

'Look, can you meet me later?' I asked.

'I don't know there's . . .'

'Will you call me, let me know?'

'OK,' she shook her head, thoughts clearing. 'OK, give me the number.'

I wrote it on the telephone pad.

'Look you'd better go,' she said quickly, 'someone might come. I'll call.'

It *was* better that way, holding her hand for a brief second, catching her eyes at the front door, not wanting to let them go.

I got into the car and drove back to the hotel. We hadn't even talked. But there was something more important than that. We now shared a secret, just the two of us, the way we had done all those years ago.

## TWENTY-ONE

In Clarky's version they had gathered in a semi-circle around him, like wolves. The woman called Lisa adjusted her spectacles and opened a notepad. He could see her scrawling his name in the top left-hand corner.

'I have no business with these people,' he told Christian. 'I wish to go back to my hotel.'

Lisa wrote something unintelligible on her pad.

'My friend,' Christian sniffed noisily, 'what can I say? Berlin is a German city again. The Americans are leaving, the Russians are leaving, your people, also – they will be going home. Our city,' he added, shaking his head up and down, 'with no one to tell us what to do.'

Clarky's mind began to register alarm.

'Always it was your Berlin, you could disband the senate, dismiss the police – your troops . . .' Christian's voice was rising, 'your airline flying in and out of our city . . .'

'You didn't object when it was bringing your people food.'

'You used us, my friend.' He wiped the spit away

163

from his mouth. 'We were the little island between you and the Russians, a means of testing the temperature. But if the bears had even growled, you'd have cooked us yourselves and shared the meal with them.'

Clarky paused for a moment, trying to take control. 'And these are your new colleagues . . .' he gestured towards the semi-circle.

'They are Germans.'

'From the East, I suppose . . . ?'

'East – West, what does it matter?'

'Not a lot.' And in that moment Clarky knew who they were. For he could read the training in their eyes, the way one professional always spots another. They were weighing him up and making a pretty good job of it, taking in his gestures, his body language, noting his breathing, giving nothing themselves. They'd let him talk for hours if he didn't shut up.

Clarky chuckled. 'And how is life in the Normannenstrasse, these days, Ladies and Gentlemen, and Herr Mielke, and the rest of your comrades? Mmm? Nothing to say?'

Lisa put down her pencil. 'The Normannenstrasse no longer belongs to State Security, Herr Clark. It is about to be given over to the German railway board. As for Herr Mielke he is currently in Moabit jail in Berlin-West.' She removed her glasses. The cheeks were flat and sallow and she didn't bother with make-up.

164

'You are in a hostel, Herr Clark,' she continued. 'Former members of the Stasi, as you used to call us, are awaiting transfer to positions in the new Republic. It is all quite legal, quite accepted. My colleagues and I . . .' she didn't look at them, 'are simply tying loose ends. Administrative matters. That is all.'

God, she was good, thought Clarky. Vintage Stasi. Well-travelled, bright, light-years from the kind of thug they used to put out in the Alexanderplatz to break up demonstrations. They were the best of the best, always had been. And she lied without even a shimmer of the eyebrows, convincing herself, even before she tried convincing him. That was training. Believe your own lies, they used to say. Believe them, run with them, act them out in your mind. Lie to children and old ladies, and the terminally sick just for practice – and soon you won't know the difference.

Hard bastards, they were – all of them.

'Good, well now we know where we stand.' Clarky produced a verbal flannel and waved it at them. 'So good to meet you, but I don't think we have anything more to say.' He put his hands on his knees, a gesture of finality.

Lisa stood up. Her hair was black and unkempt, and she had the appearance of odd bumps and angles, the kinds of shapes that East German underwear tended to produce.

'Herr Clark, we would ask you to remain here as

our guest for a while. We simply wish to clarify your identity.'

And that seemed to sum him up and dismiss him. Apparently Clarky didn't remember the rest of the little speech. He was too busy lunging insanely at the door, recalling the way the wolves threw themselves on top of him, pinning his hands and his feet, forcing the breath from his chest.

What a bloody fool, old Clarky – out so long he'd forgotten how to be frightened.

He recalled his final thought, as their boots jammed into his kidneys and his teeth bit the filthy, threadbare rug ... that they were all the same, those creatures, in their suits and ties and twinsets – with their classless, clinical disregard for life.

Heidi had taken the wheel, offering to drop Iris at the Hotel Castor. She drove fast and confidently, crossing Unter Den Linden, heading for the old Checkpoint Charlie. The buildings slept and in all directions the streetlamps hung dim and crooked against the sky. Iris couldn't help thinking it would always be East Berlin, at least in her lifetime. East would mean second-class, second-rate. As Clarky had once put it – the place they'd all pissed on from a great height.

Abruptly, Heidi turned off the Friedrichstrasse and stopped the car. She pulled a cigarette from her handbag and lit it, opening the window, watching the smoke fan out into the night.

'Christian's a shit,' she said quietly.

'I'm sorry . . . ?'

'Well, you heard him. It's not the first time he's put me down like that.' Iris considered putting an arm round her shoulders, but she hadn't much taken to Heidi.

'All men are like that, from time to time,' Iris said, trying to sound comforting.

'All men are not like Christian.' Heidi pouted, a little too long for a forty year old. She threw away the cigarette. 'Look, why don't we get drunk somewhere? Berlin has many clubs. I show you.'

'What about my friend?'

'Your friend's fine.'

Iris didn't think much of the club – and not just because she was a sceptical lady and, apart from her association with Clarky, an eminently sensible lady – but it wasn't what she'd expected.

The place was half-buried in the Pankow district of East Berlin – ten steps down from pavement level, a room of dark corners, tables encrusted with candle wax, and whispering teenagers.

Heidi looked round. A handful of teenagers looked back. She ordered rum and cokes and sighed loudly, as if to declare the conversation open.

'What is this place?' asked Iris.

'Why? You don't like it?'

'No, well . . . No, it's fine.'

'I love it,' said Heidi. 'The first boy I ever kissed, used to work behind the bar.'

'Really.'

The drinks came. Rum and ice.

'No coke today,' said the waitress. 'Tomorrow.'

Heidi raised her eyebrows. 'I brought Christian here once,' she mused. 'He also hated it. But then he likes lots of glass and chrome and bright lights and music. Western things . . .'

'And you don't?'

'Of course I do. You think just because we live in the pigsty we have never heard of the palace?'

Heidi talked like a bad English textbook.

She hunted for another cigarette. 'Often he makes me look after his clients.'

Iris said nothing.

'It's not what you think,' said Heidi. 'I do not go to bed with them. That would be very unclever.'

'Very,' agreed Iris.

Heidi drank her rum and ordered another. 'No, but take tonight for instance. Christian says, "These are important people from London, so be nice to them, make them feel at home, and if things go badly you can help smooth it all out."'

'Why did he say that about things going badly?' Iris sat up.

'I don't know. He comes in after work and he's nervous. Locks himself in the bedroom and makes phone calls for half an hour. Suddenly he comes out and says, "It's OK. There'll be no trouble." Then he starts drinking.'

'Who did he call?'

'He never tells.' Heidi drank again, swirling the ice cubes inside her mouth. 'Only tonight he leaves an address on the pad by the bed.'

'Did you ask him about it?'

'You think I'm crazy? I just remember things and store them in my little head. Like his cars and the money he never tells to the tax man. So one day if Christian makes trouble for me – maybe I make some for him.' She finished the glass.

They had locked Clarky in a box-room, airless and windowless, and now in total darkness.

Fine by him. For he felt more ashamed than harmed, his pride more damaged than his kidneys.

Once they had restrained him, they beat him up briefly and scientifically, causing maximum hurt with minimum effort. No one even had to remove their jacket.

He didn't know that Iris was sitting outside the building in Heidi's car, just a few feet away, but it wouldn't have made much difference. For nearly thirty years East and West had been separated by a few feet across the Berlin Wall. It might just as well have been another planet.

# TWENTY-TWO

Funny how you awake, knowing your mind has journeyed without you, trying to trace its path, read its records. Somewhere lost in my sleep there had been a question that I couldn't answer.

It hung there while I shaved and dressed, and took the lift to my breakfast.

And only when I had finished, with a stomach full of taste enhancers and black coffee, telling myself how comfortable it all felt could I see what was wrong.

Too easy. America was too easy. The 'Have a good stay' at Immigration, where your name is fed to the computer, and checked against every known record they possess, the whore in the lobby, Cassie, at home in the middle of the day, just when you called . . .

Martin, Martin. Maybe everyone has been watching along the route – the Russians, the Stasi, and now the Americans . . . ?'

Maybe they don't want to kill you unless they have to, unless you find out too much. You see it's not good to blow away British operatives – even ones like me. Raises a few suspicions. People start getting edgy and inquisitive. Governments have been known to protest. And maybe the traitor is close enough that the shockwave would bring even him into question.

I didn't leave my hotel room that day. I didn't even want to use the phone. But as the hours went by there was no call from Cassie.

Had she lost the number?

I told myself, don't act like a teenager, and laid down on the bed, flicking through the fifty TV channels, finding nothing.

Cassie, call me!

I must have fallen asleep for I couldn't remember if I'd seen her or dreamed it. So many times my own thoughts had tricked me, giving her image a form and a presence and a voice I thought I'd heard.

But in the half-darkness of the room, the phone rang and she said: 'I'm in the lobby.' And even after so many years I wanted to say, come up, it's me, and she'd have said, yeah it's me, too – and stayed where she was.

'I'll be right down,' I replied.

She saw me first. It had always been that way. Cassie outmanoeuvred me on all fronts. So often I would find myself a dozen mental paragraphs behind her, catching a point she'd made hours before.

She was by the bar, watching me, while I

scanned reception. And when I turned towards her she smiled, as if remembering the same things.

Cassie, come back.

We sat in the coffee shop, she in a loose cotton dress, pink and blue, the summer in her eyes. And I had to keep telling myself I didn't know her any more, and couldn't share the space she lived in.

'This is so hard,' I told her.

'I know.' She took my hand and I tried not to remember the many times she had held it.

'I left East Germany two days ago, everyone around me seemed to be dying . . . I can't even begin to tell you what that was like.' Cassie gripped my hand more tightly. 'This is unreal coming here. You. Washington.'

Someone brought me a coffee I couldn't remember ordering.

'I didn't know what happened,' she said. 'Part of it, I mean you going into Berlin. I kept asking. They kept showing me a brick wall.'

'Better not to talk about walls.'

She smiled again. It was the same picture of her that I'd carried in my head for so long. There was so much I wanted to ask, and so much I didn't want to hear. Who she'd been with, where she'd had holidays, how she'd laughed and loved without me.

Martin, you're so selfish.

'I need some help, Cassie. I need to know what happened when I left. What they said, who said it. I

172

come back after all this time – the British don't want to know me, and the KGB wants me dead.'

I told her what I could, but I held things back as well. The Berlin years had done that for me. Being close to the Stasi taught you never to trust a soul, because there's always a point where that soul will fail you, betray you – always a breaking point. You have only to find it.

'I need to think back,' she said. 'You know I'm still at Langley. I can't ask anyone there. I was ordered to stay away from you.'

'And you always obeyed orders . . .'

She caught the tiny shock of anger and the hurt spread across her face like a shadow.

'I'm sorry, Cassie . . .'

She kept holding my hand, but turned away her eyes. 'Don't think it was easy for me . . .'

'I don't. I just never knew. There were so many times when I wanted to call you – like every day.'

Her eyes came back to me. We stopped talking, and I could see her trying to frame words she knew I wouldn't like.

'You heard about Harry, didn't you?'

'Fenton? Yes . . . yes I did.' I don't think I'd ever heard him called 'Harry'. To us he'd just had a surname.

'I took him to the airport this afternoon. That's why I couldn't call before. He had to go away to Paris. Government negotiations. Troop reductions.'

'I see.'

I looked around the trim little coffee shop, with the wide-smiling waitresses, and the piped music, and thick carpets and polite patrons – and it was suddenly too much for a man who'd been locked up in East Berlin. I got up and slid on to the seat next to Cassie and held her so tightly in both arms that I felt sure she would cry out in protest and push me away.

Several minutes must have passed, while the conversations around us halted, and people stared – cakes bulging in their mouths – before I realized she was holding me just as tight.

We had dinner at a fish restaurant beside the Georgetown Canal – the last table by the water's edge, and we both laughed at that. Whenever we'd gone out we'd beaten the odds, finding theatre tickets when all the seats were sold, parking spaces when the city was jammed – all the good things, the rare things, the lucky things had come to us without effort.

'Don't count on it,' Cassie always said. And I never had. Only we both played the game, 'Well, if this happens, or that happens, then it means this or that or something else.' Letting fate make the decisions. As if it didn't.

'Tonight's just for us,' she said, after we'd sipped the wine. And it sounded like a door opening to the past. I had feared she'd be a stranger, but I think I realized then that she never could be. Time cannot take away what is real, it just dispels the illusions. Works of art are eternal. Only fakes lose their value.

'I remember so many good things,' I told her.

'You remember too much,' she replied. And the smile had returned.

A waiter took our order. Smoked salmon, sword-fish, crab cocktail.

'You didn't eat like this in East Berlin.'

'Of course we did. We were the élite, the chosen few, or in the Stasi's case, the chosen many. D'you know that more than one in five of those good East German citizens informed on their friends at some time in their lives?'

She lifted her glass and I poured.

'I read the files.'

'Of course you did.'

'They still have one on you.' She pointed over the Potomac in the direction of Langley.

'What does it say?'

'I wasn't allowed to read it for a long time.'

'So how did you?'

'I got promoted.' Cassie put down her glass. 'It says they have lingering doubts about you.'

'Oh?'

'The British story, never tolerated close examin-ation. You were one of those suspected of betraying the East German networks, you had a car accident, your personal life was not exactly . . .'

'Our personal life . . .'

175

'Yours for the purposes of the file.' She breathed deeply, moving aside her elbows to let the waiter deposit a plate. 'You were an ideal candidate to have been turned.'

'But Langley never accepted that version?'

'Not completely.'

'Why?'

'Because I didn't accept it. Only every time I wanted a check run through British Intelligence I was turned down. You were "hands-off" to everyone. If we'd even so much as whistled at you, the British would have screamed the house down . . .'

'And Fenton never told you?'

'He told me to forget all about you, and this was business . . .'

'But you married the man and still . . .' I stopped, suddenly no longer wanting to pursue that line.

'Yes I married him, and our business was separate and that's all I can tell you.'

'You mean there's more.'

'I don't know.'

She looked exhausted and scared, almost as if she'd dug up a coffin and peered inside. 'Can we drop this for a moment?'

I put down my fork.

'Tell me how you've been, Cassie.'

'OK.'

'No better than that?'

'Yes fine.' She nodded. 'Absolutely. What can I say? Fine, really.'

'Fine' had never been a very enthusiastic adjective in Cassie's vocabulary, but I wasn't going to pursue it. I told her about my work in East Berlin, about the atmosphere in the Stasi, the constant threat briefings, the high state of alert, the fear that an attack by the West was imminent.

She nodded, but her eyes looked down at the table, and her mind was somewhere well away.

When the meal was cleared, we ordered coffee and then strolled along the footpath beside the canal. The lights from the restaurant gave us long shadows and strange reflections in the water. Cassie took my arm, just as if she'd never let it go.

'I know what you're thinking,' she said. 'But Fenton's not a bad man. Really he's not. He tries so hard to understand me.'

'And does he?'

She shook her head. 'I shouldn't be talking to you like this.' We crossed under a bridge and stood still in the darkness.

'You know it was he who persuaded me to defect?'

'And Keen?'

'Keen as well. But I'll need to talk to Fenton, I mean Harry – when he comes back.'

'Why? He just did what Keen told him.'

'I don't know that.'

And even in the darkness I could see the look she threw me – straight and sharp – the clearest of warnings to go no further.

I drove her back to Brandywine Street, and held the door open and hurried back inside the car, so she wouldn't have to make excuses for not inviting me in. I said I'd call her in the morning, wondering at what point I would have to tell her that Fenton was high on my list of suspects.

# TWENTY-THREE

Long before I fell asleep, I had a dream. I was in East Berlin again, but everyone spoke English with American accents, the shops were full, the food was wonderful and you could go anywhere you wanted. It was a dream that jumbled the past with the present, friends with enemies, different continents and politics. But it was still East Berlin.

She called me before dawn. Three, four a.m. – I don't recall that exactly. Nor the words she used. Only the way she said them.

It took about ten minutes to reach the house. Concealed lighting illuminated the front path, only that night the stars could have done it on their own. The door wasn't locked. I found myself in the hall, with the smell of fresh flowers and the hardwood floors polished and smoothed as if designed for serious accidents.

Cassie appeared from the sitting room. I could see she hadn't been to bed. Same clothes but there were more creases in them, and the eyes were hooded with tiredness.

We sat on stools in the kitchen and she made coffee.

'I tried calling him – Harry – in Paris but he wasn't at the hotel he normally stays at. And usually I don't call, but this time after we'd talked . . .'

'So you left a message . . .'

'There was no booking. I waited up and rang the Paris embassy, and they didn't even know he was coming. They had no idea. Nothing.'

She paused and I waited for her to tell me more. Cassie was so quick and so bright. She wouldn't have left it at that.

She toyed with her coffee mug. 'In the end I called a hotel in Berlin. He stayed there once or twice. It's in the East – you know . . .' she broke off. 'Of course you do. I asked for Harry and they put me straight through, and you know what I did?'

'You put the phone down.'

She got up. 'I heard his voice and I couldn't talk to him, couldn't say a word.'

I sat without moving, hearing the world at half speed, in the distance, a siren.

'There's a Lufthansa flight, leaves Dulles in the morning, goes via Frankfurt.' She picked up the cups, tidy and efficient and put them in the dishwasher. 'I've got time off. Harry and I were going to . . .' she shrugged. 'Well, now we're not.'

'I'll ride with you,' I said, 'but I'll go to London

180

first. I have to see Keen. None of this is fitting into place.'

'What d'you mean?'

'Last time I got to England, someone was trying to kill me. In Berlin everyone I talked to got themselves murdered. Here, there's peace and quiet and I haven't even had a lousy meal.'

She smiled. 'You see, I look after you.'

'No, I'm serious,' I replied.

'So am I.'

We didn't talk much after that. I seemed to have the feeling that we'd both said too much, but I didn't know why.

Outside the night lapsed into day and by then she had a case packed beside the door, and we drove to my hotel, as the traffic built up around us.

She turned on the car radio and we learned about two shootings in the south-east of the city, and a fire, and then way, way down there was the president's schedule. And I thought, after East Berlin, that they'd got their priorities in order.

We stood in line at the airport for well over an hour, waiting for tickets and check in, before climbing into those lounges-on-wheels that crawl like giant insects across the runways.

I don't know what made me turn round. The doors were closing and through the glass, you could see back into the airport, and there was a face at that window – that I'd really hoped never to see again. Unless it was dead or dying or in terminal pain. But it wasn't in any of those states. Kirsch was gesturing and shaking his head up and down, like some sort of grotesque clown. Only it was he who was laughing – not me.

# TWENTY-FOUR

Iris, there were times that night when you said you lost your nerve, parked outside a strange apartment block in the run-down streets of Berlin's Prenzlauer Berg. Moments of panic and uncertainty as the extent of the danger appeared to her. And yet, how could it have been otherwise?

She had no experience of intrigue or deception, beyond the kind practised in any office. She had managed Service records, not operations, and her one moment of excitement was said to have been in the back seat of a West End cinema with an officer from Counter-intelligence. An event that indicated agility, rather than presence of mind.

They had been there ten minutes before Heidi wanted to leave.

'It is stupid,' she said. 'He is not even here. We cannot just sit all night.'

They were both silent. The way Iris told it, there were better ways of spending an evening. Peace was breaking out everywhere, Communist governments lying all over the place, dead as dinosaurs — and she was sitting in a car at two o'clock in the morning because an old boyfriend might have got himself into trouble.

Heidi turned on the car radio and rocked gently from side to side, humming a tune.

'Sit still Heidi. I'm trying to think.'

'Nothing to think,' said Heidi. 'It's late. I wish to sleep.'

She began to pout again. A bit like an overgrown doll. Someone must have told her once that she was a brainless bimbo, because she seemed to want to act like one. And yet it can't always have been that way. Spectacular body, nice eyes, sense of humour — quite enough to enthrall most of the civilized world. Only she'd ended up with Christian.

Iris shut her eyes for a moment, but she could feel Heidi freeze, feel the shockwave go through her. And then she was staring hard through the dirty windscreen and it had to be Christian, about forty yards away — already out of the building. Even in the light from the streetlamps, you could make out the sharp suit, the heavy shoulders, the confidence.

We should stop him, thought Iris, but he was moving faster than she could think. Almost immediately the Renault seemed to lurch forward, turning into a maze of darkened side-streets, and she knew she couldn't follow.

'Heidi, where's he going?'

'There's a club.'

'There's always a club . . .'

'Christian owns a place. It's called King George. Wilmersdorf.'

'Doesn't he go home?'

'Not till late. Doesn't need to. The girls at the club look after him, if he feels like it. We don't do it much any more.'

It was a matter-of-fact statement. Just the way things were. But you could see she had cried about it once upon a time, and wasn't going to cry again.

By that time they were both exhausted – had to be – and even though Iris had promised herself to stay awake, and think it through, maybe she just closed her eyes for a few moments – Heidi too. However it happened, neither of them noticed the car that slid quietly to a halt about thirty yards behind them, or the men inside, or the uniforms and the holstered automatics.

Clarky said they began on him, almost immediately after Christian had left. And it seemed for all their sophistication that so little had changed. Two of them with rolled-up shirt-sleeves, desk lamp in the eyes, one behind the chair . . . Clarky was counting off the props, and wondering how they would start, before he remembered it was all for him.

They say that interrogations never go the way you think. Once you start playing with a human mind, it starts to play back. Even the straight-forward and honest become devious and silly.

Pressure changes a mind, not just forcing it to open or close, but to alter shape. Sometimes it never returns to what it was. Not when it's damaged.

I had watched this happen myself. Shy people becoming talkative, the garrulous clamming up. You can explore the inner workings of a mind for a lifetime, finding no answers, no short cuts, chasing moods and whims that vanish before you can locate their cause.

Which is why, perhaps, the interrogators are often in a hurry. Not because they're under threat, but because if you don't make progress fast, you may not make any at all.

These, though, seemed to take an age, preparing themselves, laying out the hypodermics and a couple of surgical instruments that Clarky hadn't seen before, just letting the tension build, ignoring him, as if he had nothing to do with the procedure. When they were ready, they sat in front of him, two of them, and asked the question that, in all the wide world, he said he had least expected.

I have often wondered how Iris did what she did, because it isn't every Englishwoman of a certain age, who nods off in a street in East Berlin, finds a uniformed policeman, shining a torch in her eyes, and doesn't go round the bend with fright.

And what made her get Heidi to translate such a pack of blatant, ill-conceived lies, that the German lady was too stunned even to argue; how her husband had kidnapped her daughter, how the daughter was somewhere in that block over there, how the man took drugs and the child, even now, even at this god-forsaken hour in this god-forsaken city, was in mortal danger.

Say what you like about Germans, but when moral outrage is triggered, they don't mess around. The policeman's jaw seemed to set rigid and Iris swears the hair stood up on his crown, although it was probably the wind. At any rate, he was breathing fire into his radio and within minutes, the street seemed to fill with sirens and flashing lights and men in riot gear.

Only then did they seem organized – a unit, under clear command, disciplined and prac-tised. And for the first time Iris could identify the steel that had once held East Germany in line. You're good at this, she thought. Give you a target, give you a cause – and you'll smash your way through.

They didn't make much noise, but within seconds the first people were being herded out in their pyjamas and dressing-gowns, frightened and bleary-eyed. And yet there wasn't the shock or panic there might have been elsewhere. In the old people's eyes, Iris could read something close to resignation as the old images of Berlin mingled with the new. A few teenagers argued, a boy in a T-shirt, an earring, spiky hair, carping and biting like a terrier. And they shut him up, clouting him on the neck with a truncheon, quick and brutal, so that the others could get the idea as well.

Through all this Heidi sat in the car, floundering, unable to understand the events around her. So she didn't see the four who were led out separately from the others and put straight in a van, their hands cuffed behind their back, nor the officer who led the laughing, crying, stooping figure of Clarky from the building. He sat on the kerb, and Iris ran over to cover him with her arms and her body.

Clarky was shaking from the cold and his words came in short, staccato bursts.

'They asked me how long I had worked in the KGB,' he kept saying. 'Me in that place!' And then he would whimper a little, quite out of control, until Iris got him back in the car and held his head in her hands, quite uncertain, and unaccountably fearful of the things he was saying.

# TWENTY-FIVE

We were way out over the Atlantic by the time the walls began tumbling down and Cassie would speak to me.

Tales of Fenton.

And I suppose I had wanted him to be cold and pathetic, like so many in this business, mistreating her, worse still, boring her – a drip, a bigot – so that I could emerge and offer her a life. But it was different.

She gave me the good and the bad – and their life was like a board game, with each having different rules. They could sit together and play for a while, but they couldn't ever finish. Time and again he would seek to impose his regulations. She would counter with hers. In the end they shared the board and the squares and nothing else. The moment they moved they risked clashing.

Sometimes, she told me, they had managed to pretend. Tiptoe around in the safe areas. Talk of friends and holidays and politics, stage-manage some peace and contentment. But eventually they would blunder into a forbidden zone, because, she said, you are who you are – and you can't play games forever.

And yet, there was affection, like that between a brother and sister. But it wasn't enough. To Fenton marriage meant total immersion. He had to fill her thoughts and her life, each spare moment, each day off, each evening. He needed a single haven and a single truth – and she needed many. And so the free spirit inside her had been dying.

There comes a time, she told me, when you look at who you have become – both of you, together. Do we make each other happy, do we help each other develop? Do we go forward or stand still?

Dinner came in its plastic packets, but I hardly noticed it, absorbed and immobilized by her story.

At times she couldn't help laughing, touching my arm, holding it, recalling sensations I had long forgotten. She told of Fenton's obsession with tidiness, how he had refused to invite in a guest with muddy boots, how the man had been obliged to remove his footwear at the door, how Fenton had vacuumed the carpet late into the night, and gone to bed, cursing the world's untidiness.

He would brush his hair, before washing it, spend hours sewing on missing buttons, removing stains from his trousers.

'I can't believe it doesn't matter to you,' he would tell her when she ventured to laugh at him. 'You should do this too. You can't go around not looking your best.'

Diets had been the next fad. One morning he had watched her with unusual attention as she got out of bed. She had half expected him to pull her back for a cuddle, but it wasn't his way. 'You've put on weight,' he told her. 'You should get into shape, take some exercise.' And later that morning she had watched him struggling into an old pair of jeans, that he had long ago outgrown. But she had said nothing. That was *her* way. No unkindness in Cassie – only the sense of fun for which he seemed to have no use.

Some things they shared. The long hours, the emotional expenditure, the absences neither was authorized to explain. But it was she who did the looking after. Fenton could manage his work, but not the frustrations, the let-downs, the pressure points where a secret life impinges so badly on a normal one. She, it was, who had to coax him and offer comfort. She who made the excuses and changed the plans and papered over the cracks. And if, sometimes, she wept for the disappointments of her own – then she did so by herself.

I found it hard to picture that life as we rode the clouds in darkness, no longer in her world or mine, but somehow transiting between the two.

In East Germany I had lived in a cushioned cave. What did I know about marriage? Most of my energies had been devoted to work or to sex, acting my role, trying, I now recall, to stay alive for the day when I would be needed – the day, of course, that had never come.

My knowledge of human relations was many years old, covered in dust, stored in darkness. My feelings were brittle and ill-defined. If I possessed a roadmap it was long out of date.

All this, Cassie seemed to realize, as she stared at me on the plane to Europe.

Even then, without question or discussion, I believe we both accepted the ties that still bound us.

So maybe none of this was about a search for a traitor, and the pattern of deep deception and the manoeuvrings of men in bunkers under the streets of Berlin. Maybe it was just about her and me, and the kind of future neither of us could then foresee.

Dawn came to Frankfurt and brought us with it. And it seemed to me unaccountably sad that the journey had ended, and we were no longer strapped in side by side, with all our histories to tell.

We sat in a coffee bar in A complex or B or C – they're probably all the same – and she explained what she would do.

'I'll find Harry,' she said. 'I have to sort things out first with him. I can't think about us until then. However crazy it is, I owe him that.'

It was her way, kind and fair, and not wanting to

hurt. And I couldn't find it, even in my selfish heart, to wish her different.

I finished the coffee and paid the bill.

'Thank you,' she said. She had always thanked me, even for the smallest things.

'Why did he go to Berlin, Cassie?'

'I couldn't begin to tell you.' And she got up quickly, her eyes pleading with me not to ask why she had lied.

## TWENTY-SIX

So she left for Berlin, and waved to me a small carefree wave, like a society belle, as if to say, I have no worries, no fears, life is a party. And that, too, was a lie.

Cassie, you always left me with puzzles, as if you were testing me. Anyone else, and I would have fought and protested, and backed them into a corner. But I can't with you. I can't pursue you, can't question you, for, at the slightest sign of pressure you slip out of reach. I can only wait for you to turn and walk towards me. I must trust you completely, for you will accept nothing less, and nor should you. Why are you so vital to my life? Years have passed and I still ask the same question and find no answer.

I went back to the coffee shop and bought a sheaf of newspapers and watched the travellers in transit.

From the departure board I could see that Cassie's plane had taken off. What had she meant about looking after me? And why had I been so safe in America? From being an endangered species I was fast becoming a protected one. In London with Clarky. In Washington.

For a while it suited someone to keep me alive, and give me the illusion of being comfortable and secure. Suddenly I seemed to have friends and helpers – and that made me more nervous than ever.

I had a vision of someone smiling a beautiful smile and speaking fine words, and pushing a knife into my heart, so deftly and so skilfully that I would hardly know the end had come.

If you keep travelling long enough, you stop noticing the differences. Already America had blurred into Europe, Germany into Britain and I was feeling almost nostalgic for the little room I'd filled just three days before in East Berlin.

I'd heard of it happening. Long-serving prisoners, finally released, unable to leave their cell, crying at the windows, scared of the life outside. But I never thought it would be me.

As the years dragged past me in the GDR the hunger to leave had intensified. True I'd assembled some of the baggage and furniture that anchor people to their dwellings – clothes, books, records, toothbrush – and some people would have called that home. But it hadn't been mine.

And yet, was I now close to missing the place? Frau Ansbach's overweight, oversexed features. The petty little Glicks, informing their heads off, constantly worried that someone was doing it to them. Dortmunder, who'd cultivated being weird and silent, because it was the closest he could come to a personality. What a menagerie! And where were they now?

In the late evening I made my way to Oxford, surprised at the silence around me. The summer vacation had struck the university and all but emptied it. Only a few people were on the streets – earnest, probably eccentric, immersed no doubt within their texts of Old Norse, or logarithms, or laws of Tort. I wonder if they realized that education was equipping them solely for life in a library. People would label them brilliant because no one would understand a thing they said and, for all time, they'd receive the benefit of the doubt – a commodity only ever traded in Britain.

The college was more than half dead. In the porter's lodge, a blue-suited pensioner sat asleep at his desk. Just a handful of lights burned in the quadrangle and I crossed unnoticed towards Keen's staircase.

And maybe they don't lock doors in Oxford, or maybe there was no need. But it reminded me of Old Moore's place in East Berlin – cold, despite the summer warmth, empty despite the clutter in all directions.

Keen had gone too. Most likely a Service car would have arrived with a Service chauffeur to help him so politely on his way, carrying his bag, pointing with his walking stick, giggling stupidly at all around him?

I didn't know and in any case I was suddenly so tired, standing there, with the light from the gas-lamps, coming through the windows. There was little point in rummaging through the room, or looking for Keen, or making a nuisance of myself.

I sat on the floor for a while and closed my eyes and for some reason, thought about my mother. Maybe it was her connection with Keen, maybe just the helplessness and the child that some of us can never shake off. She would have been so shocked at the life I'd led, shocked by the truth, the shattered principles, the forgotten precepts. 'That's not the way you were brought up,' I could hear her saying. 'We never taught you to tell lies or go round cheating people. Couldn't you have just married someone nice and had children . . .' Even so my mother had owned a glint in her eye that spoke volumes about the way she really thought. She had always loved the unusual and unpredictable; journeys far away, movement and light and music. Maybe she had once been Cassie, but now I would never know.

In any case her memory seemed to give me strength. Only it showed how desperate I had become that, in that moment, I was looking to a dead person, for the impetus and the energy and the will to carry on.

By the time I re-crossed the quadrangle, the porter had woken up and was boiling his kettle. As he saw me he came to the window and slid aside an opening.

'College is closed, sir.'

'I know.'

'What was it you was looking for?'

'A person.'

'Person? Not too many of those here just now.'

I went round the side and entered the porter's lodge and I couldn't help scanning the pigeon holes for mail, only I saw instantly that Keen's was empty.

'I did say we was closed.' It was a broad Oxfordshire accent and a firm tone of voice and I could just hear him saying to the male students, 'No women in your room after eleven, sir. Told you that before, haven't I? Rules are rules.'

'I was looking for Professor Keen.'

For some reason he pushed a cup of tea across the shiny counter and packed away the milk and sugar in a tiny fridge beneath it.

He wore a waistcoat with a gold chain spanning the pockets. On it was a watch that he took out and examined.

'It's late, sir. The professor won't be coming back tonight.'

'D'you know when he is coming back?'

He looked at me as if the question were somehow irrelevant and sipped his tea.

'I've always liked the professor,' he said, staring hard into the teacup.

'I haven't.'

'No I suppose not.' He ran a hand through his grey, curly hair and his face seemed to cloud over with memories. 'Never been a warm sort of fellow, if you know what I mean. Well, none of us was during the fighting . . .'

'You knew him in the war?'

The porter didn't answer straightaway. He searched in his jacket pockets, not finding what he wanted.

'I'd kill for a cigarette,' he said abruptly, smiling gold and white teeth.

'I'd kill anyway,' I replied, and in that instant my thoughts seemed to brake to a sudden halt, feeling the shiver of ancient recognition, realizing I'd said it without thinking – the Berlin identification code, half uttered by the porter, completed by me.

'I'd kill anyway,' I repeated under my breath.

'I thought you would,' he said quietly and shook his head as if marvelling at some old prophecy come true. 'The professor knew you'd come by, along with all the others. He was good like that, practical man, none of that head-in-the-clouds nonsense you get from some of them.'

'What others came by?'

'Different shapes and sizes.'

I thought he was after money, so I removed my

wallet, but he looked offended and brushed my hand aside and hurried away down the stairs into the basement. I could only stand there, thinking how clever Keen had become, sense of timing intact, and a little network, squirrelled together and operating wherever he went. Keen always had his people – the quiet men and women, unobtrusive, loyal, I expect, because it never occurred to them to be otherwise. The best reason of all.

The porter returned with a white envelope and handed it to me.

'Better go now, sir, if I were you.'

'Right. Thanks for the tea.'

'Pleasure, sir.'

He held out his hand and it was dry and firm and trustworthy – the kind of hand I hadn't been offered in four years of shaking them in East Germany – where they'd all been damp and weak like the people who owned them.

'Dear Martin.'

Reading the letter in the hotel lobby and on the stairs up to my room.

'Not going well I'm afraid. A few unexpected complications. Feel we should talk.'

Turning now into the corridor, wondering if Keen had giggled all the time he'd been writing this.

'Why don't you come up to Northumberland one

afternoon, have tea, go for a walk along the beach?'

Key in my door. Light on. Maid must have turned down the bed.

'Come tomorrow, why don't you? Best not to hang around.'

And then I could see Kirsch lying broken on the floor beside the bed, holding the gun he said he didn't know how to use, his eyes lolling sightless in their sockets. Never less at home than in this soft, understated little bedroom, next to the seat of scholarship, about which he would have known nothing.

He had died, it seemed, much as he had lived, with the grease on his forehead and that expression of amiable nastiness, as if he was really so very misunderstood, and was only being cruel to be kind.

He was propped awkwardly against the bed, evidently the position in which he had fallen. I bent down and looked for a wound, but couldn't see one.

Kirsch had been dropped by an expert, probably with a blow to any of a handful of pressure points on the face or neck or over the heart. And he wouldn't have liked that much. Kirsch had prided himself on being the State's best thug, and had had to die to find out he wasn't. I could do nothing about the anger that surged inside me, for it was clear he hadn't suffered anything like as much as

I'd intended. His would have been a short and shocking death, devoid of the kind of pain he had meted out to his own victims. Whatever it was, it wasn't justice.

My bag had been opened and I began to fill it rapidly with the few things I had. Not a good idea to stay around with the mortal remains of Oskar Kirsch, who would quickly become as much of a problem in death as he had been during his short, unattractive life.

I picked up Keen's letter from the floor. It must have fallen there when I'd discovered the body. In that instant the phone rang, and I couldn't help lifting the receiver.

'Hallo, old boy,' said the voice. Only Keen talked like that to me.

'It's Martin,' I said stupidly.

'I know.'

'How?'

'Doesn't matter. What is important is that you leave the hotel now. No forwarding address, settle in cash, get out.'

'Look here. There's a . . .'

'It'll be taken care of. Clear? Right. Get yourself up here sometime tomorrow afternoon.'

Keen hung up and I stood looking at the receiver. Keen knew, knew about Kirsch, knew I was in a hotel. God knows what else he had found out, or done, or said. What sort of stupid and pointless game was being played around me? Didn't they know it was over, the Cold War, the dark war, all the dying in back streets and hotels – the world run by arrogant misfits in offices that weren't even supposed to exist?

## TWENTY-SEVEN

In the end Clarky calmed down, but in Iris's account she said he never returned to his old ways.

'He got very Polish on me,' she observed. 'All moody and sad and thoughtful, waking me up in the middle of the night, wanting it, that sort of thing.'

It was as if Clarky's former self had been locked out and was battering to get back in. For there were flashes of humour, and intelligence – a quip, a wink. But the eyes had shaded over and dulled. Clarky seemed to be wearing a notice that said, 'Gone Away'.

'We didn't talk much that day,' said Iris. 'Not after he got away from the Stasi people. He wanted to know about Heidi but he didn't tell *me* anything. And then he sort of mooched around till the evening. I was about to go to bed. To be frank I was a bit fed up – with him, with all that stuff. I wouldn't have minded going home, but he suddenly says, "We're going out, get your coat," and so we did.'

They drove the yellow Beetle to Wilmersdorf –

and Iris knew then they were heading for King George – Christian's club. Clarky had gone quiet because he'd been planning his revenge, and quite suddenly, Iris didn't like that idea.

'Clarky, why don't we . . . ?' But the look as he parked the car was quite enough to silence her.

Like Christian the outside was cheap and over-done. A neon dancing girl stood on the roof, offering her breasts to the sky, red lights flickered in upstairs windows, the door was black and locked.

Clarky rang the bell and a spyhole opened. The door swung inwards. A girl in high heels and little else led them to a table.

'It was one of those cat houses, I s'pose you'd call it,' said Iris. 'Lots of dim lighting, and everyone staring and sizing each other up for the next trick. They put us in an alcove, which suited Clarky fine, 'cos I think he wanted to see and not be seen, and the girls left us alone once they sighted me.'

By all accounts, or rather by Iris's, it was a ludicrously unexciting show. Two girls pretended to fondle each other in a bubble bath, a couple pretended to have sex on a satin sheet, and the only person there who wasn't pretending – a shy, balding little fellow in the audience, who'd opened his zip and thrust both hands between his legs – was ejected amid loud cries of 'shame' and 'scandal'.

It was in the first interval that Christian

appeared. There could be no doubt he was boss, the way he distributed smiles like pennies to the poor – a pat on a bottom, a stroke of the cheek, the touch of ownership for each of the girls. I pay you, therefore I take you.

He looked around the room, but it was too dark to make anyone out. Clarky didn't move, watching his quarry, as the man made for the back rooms, where the club would rake in the real money. Ten minutes went by, the show re-started, girl wrapped snake round her, thirty minutes, and still he didn't move. What are you going to do Clarky, she wondered? Are you going to hit him here?

The two of them watched in silence as the acts fluttered and twirled in front of them and the clientele sat on the edge of their seats, either for reasons of hygiene or in expectation of improving their view.

The strange thing, Iris said later, was that they had managed to take sex *out* of the show. The girls on the floor looked bored and distracted. They had done it all day. They did it all night. For the amount of passion involved, they might as well have been doing their washing.

And then Clarky had gone, and even with his back pain, and his exhaustion, and his mood that seemed to plummet so fast downhill, she was amazed at how quickly he moved.

Evidently it had gone like this. Clarky forcing his

way into the corridor, past the little shrieks of surprise and all the bare, restraining arms, some wanting to pull him in, others push him out. A couple of doors forced, a couple more heartfelt screams, and then he finds Christian, sitting on a bed with an Asian girl, being 'tended' as they say in polite society – which this wasn't.

So he hauls him upright, trousers still round his ankles, swipes him two or three times around the mouth, to tell him what's coming and drags him out into the back courtyard. And there, on this damp summer night in Wilmersdorf, we have only Clarky's account to go on.

He had tried, he said, not to beat Christian completely senseless, but he didn't feel much like holding back. After all he'd worked hard and close with Christian in the old days, when they had behaved like animals, run together, hidden together and pulled the thorns from each other's paws.

So to Clarky, being shopped by his friend, being led to some Stasi safe house in East Berlin and being worked over and half frightened to death by a collection of has-been thugs, was something less than 'nice' and could not 'exactly' be glossed over.

British Intelligence has always been reticent about acts of revenge. The subject of memos no one ever wanted to write, of briefings that never really took place. Revenge, someone said, was like masturbation – everyone did it, but you rather hoped they would grow out of it.

So there probably wasn't good, official justification for removing most of Christian's front teeth and kicking him in most of the painful areas the body so obligingly offers – but it would have been churlish not to talk to him before leaving.

Clarky balances Christian's upper half against a drainpipe and asks why. He had expected the usual stories about blackmail – wives and girlfriends and spare, half-fathered children being threatened and beaten about unless he co-operated – but that wasn't Christian's version.

To Clarky it was more ominous than that. Christian had spat and coughed a bit, but he had been quite lucid – fed up, he said, with all the different sides and manoeuvrings and intrigues. Where, he asked, had been the place for ordinary people?

'Well, if they had any coherent thoughts at all, your Stasi friends used to lock them up or shoot them along the Wall. Or have you forgotten?' Clarky asks.

'*Na ja*. This we know,' says Christian as if he's just discovered the New Truth. 'But it was all about governments playing with governments. Our side was interested only in this. Was there anything we did that made life a little better for anyone else?'

Clarky couldn't, apparently, find a ready answer to that.

'You see,' says Christian, adding 'my friend,' as a painful afterthought. 'You see, what did we ever find out? A troop unit was moving, a new missile was being brought in, a member of the Politburo was fucking someone he shouldn't. Did that ever put food in people's stomachs?'

'It wasn't that simple.'

'It is now.' Christian coughs again. 'Half of Germany is going to be unemployed. When the re-unification comes they will close all the factories in the East. Now is the time for all Germans to look after each other . . .'

'So that's why you fed me to the Stasi.'

Christian looks desolate, even more desolate than a man with blood all over his face, very few teeth and bruises coming up nicely over the eyes.

'They say, "We only wish to talk to Herr Clark. Few questions. Nothing more." '

'Why did they ask me if I had been in the KGB?'

'This also I know. Believe me there is great confusion. They do not know who they have. They have lost files, lost people. It is most dangerous, most tense.'

Clarky helps Christian to his feet and holds the door open for him to go inside.

'Please, Clarky, I cannot go like this. I would lose too much respect. The girls, the clients. It is hard enough . . .'

So Clarky, it seems, leaves him where he is, fetches Iris from the velvet alcove, ducks past swaying breasts and knowing smiles and drives back to the hotel.

*   *   *

For an hour or two they lay together in darkness, not speaking, listening to the city quieten around them.

And then Clarky got out of bed and sat on the side, much as a small child might visit its mother for comfort in the dead of night, and he told Iris what he'd done.

## TWENTY-EIGHT

For a moment – for just one moment I felt released,
standing in the clear northern sunshine in the early
morning. The sea was tamed, the wind hardly
bothered, the green coastline of Northumberland
rising and falling in fields and clumps of trees –
and the night train from the south so thankfully
behind me.

If I could have turned then to Cassie and said,
'Look at this – just look,' it would have been
enough. We could have left Keen to his own
devices, consigned Schmidt permanently to his
bunker in Potsdam, marched unencumbered into
our future together. That's what I meant about a
moment of release.

I got back in the taxi and we followed the coast
road towards the clouds. Keen had said I'd be
found and brought in. Best not to give directions,
old thing. Take the A1 south from Berwick. Keep
going. Piece of cake.

I'd forgotten how the British official likes to talk.
The more important the matter – the sillier and
more childish the expression. Like police talking

211

about criminals as 'chappies' or 'Charlies' or 'Johnnies'. Everyone so busy playing things down, they'd forgotten how to get turned on.

Germans were the other way, of course. It all mattered to them. Every last gasp.

'You'll be wanting to see the Holy Island.' The driver spoke for the first time. He wore glasses that covered half his face.

'Why would I want to do that?'

'Wetlands.'

I turned round to look at him. 'I beg your pardon.'

His face broke apart. 'Birds,' he said. 'Finest breeding grounds in Europe. Greylag geese, redshanks, bar-tailed godwits.'

'I see.'

We turned left off the main road, which sank away towards the sea, winding and turning past fields and hedgerows, through a level crossing, the six-colour sky filling the frame. Blue and light green and shards of orange, jumbled like a child's painting.

The driver had picked up speed and as we came to the causeway I could see why. The water was already lapping at the sides of the road and I remember thinking the tide must come in fast here, and isn't there only one way on to the island?

He spoke as if I'd asked the question. 'Only got four minutes from now and after that the causeway's underwater for about six hours. See those little huts?' He pointed to a couple of boxes on stilts. 'Every year some half-dozen tourists get stranded and have to leave their cars.' He turned full face towards me. 'They never believe us when we tell them it's dangerous.'

We curved towards the island, the front wheels already throwing up the spray. And then I realized how easy I'd made it for them – the train to Berwick, the single taxi waiting there, the amiable Scottish fellow, 'You'll be wanting to see the Holy Island,' said with all the carelessness of the true deceiver.

And quite suddenly we were off the damp sandflats and on to Lindisfarne, that pile of sacred rocks where ancient lookouts must have watched with horror as the Vikings landed in search of treasure and slaves. And I knew which I was.

In a courtyard now, two men in suits and close haircuts attending, the same stalwarts who could have come from East Berlin or East London. Plenty of muscle and all the rapid, conditioned reflexes that you get these days on most medium-priced robots.

One of them opened the door and ushered me out, and way over his shoulder I looked for the road back to the mainland. Only it wasn't there any more, reclaimed once again by the tides, with just a series of poles in the sand to mark its trajectory – the route, they say, that the pilgrims of old once travelled.

*     *     *

In the speed of it all I have the vaguest recollection of a street close to the monastery, a peasant cottage, and the sense of professionals, telling me by virtue of their presence, that this was serious.

Keen giggled in the doorway, his long grey hair caught and twisted by the wind.

He took me inside, bowing low under wooden beams. A kitchen, a boiling kettle, just the two of us, with the guardians left outside so as not to disturb.

Then come the words of cheerful welcome, like wrapping paper around a present. Peel it away, all the layers, quickly now – and you'll find out what he's done.

He potters around, making noise. 'Thanks for coming. Please sit. Tea all right? Milk? Got some lemon if you prefer . . .'

Through the window I see one of his boys talking into a portable radio. How many are there? And why so many? They hadn't been there in Oxford.

Keen placed a tray on the kitchen table and followed my gaze through the window.

'Mind if we hang on for a moment? Just waiting for a guest, and then we can all get started.'

In the distance I could hear the beating of a helicopter.

Keen ignores it. 'Weather's been a bit unsettled last couple of days. Looks like it's clearing up, though.' He peers towards the sky. 'Sorry to bring you all the way up here. Bit of a hideaway of mine really. One road in, one road out, lots of open sea, the sort of thing our watchers seem to like. Thought I'd retire here one day.'

The noise of the helicopter was suddenly monstrous, as if it had settled on the chimney pot.

Two of the guardians hurried around the side of the house, out of sight and I look at Keen, thinking, You're not out of it after all, as I'd imagined – with your study in Oxford and your books and the way you talk of life, as if it's history.

The helicopter's rotor had been cut, and we both listened for the door and the guest to come through it.

I recall being so certain of learning something I didn't want to know. Odd how you spend a life trying to acquire information and then have no more cherished desire than to get rid of it, forget it, pretend it was never there.

Sitting at the table with Keen and his teapot, I would, looking back, have settled for almost any deal except the one that walked through the door, his torso in leather flying jacket, a silk scarf at his neck, his mind full of the deceits and falsehoods that had dominated so many years of my life.

They were looking for my reaction – both of them. But I gave them little to go on. No expression of surprise, or disgust and yet I felt both.

Herr Schmidt lowered his bulk on to the tweedy

armchair, and I seem to remember hoping it was as uncomfortable as it looked.

By that time, of course, they already had plans for me. But my own seem rooted in that moment, that cloudy morning on Lindisfarne, when I realized, for the first time, that the whole thing had gone too far.

# TWENTY-NINE

Schmidt didn't get offered any tea. By then it was a
different kind of meeting. Keen, no longer vague
and hospitable, standing up by the mantelpiece,
holding forth about German politics.

He took us by a back road into the Cold War, the
way the alliance with Russia had finally gone sour,
the way we'd kept our eye on the wrong target.

'All so busy making sure we'd put the Nazis to
bed, we forgot about the East.' His mouth widened
as if he somehow found that funny, but his eyes
didn't. Focused eyes – on me and Schmidt.

'Same thing now,' Keen went on. 'We're still set
on burying the Reds, when it's the Hard Right that
needs our attentions. All the nationalists, the anti-
Jews, the anti-Slavs, just the same as they always
were.'

He looked as if he expected a response, but it was
only his way.

'Of course, the ideology never mattered a damn.
People didn't realize that. It was only the formula
for taking power. If it turned out to be the wrong
one, well then you chucked it away and picked up

another. They'll pick up any label that's going if it works.'

I turned away and looked out of the window, and he droned on a little longer about how, once again, the world was hurrying down the nearest drain. And then he stopped.

'Martin?'

Outside it had begun to rain. The guardians were sheltering beneath coloured umbrellas. I turned to face them both.

'What's he doing here?' I asked, pointing at Schmidt.

And then they both smiled, for it was clear I'd acted the part and said the lines, just the way they'd planned.

Schmidt didn't seem to mind being ushered upstairs.

Keen poured fresh tea, as if only we English were allowed to drink it.

'D'you know his name?' he pointed towards the ceiling.

'I call him Schmidt for want of anything better.'

'So do we.' Keen sat at the table. 'It also has the benefit of being his real name.' He giggled. 'What I said earlier is perfectly true. Now the Wall's down, East Germans are changing sides, the way we change shirts. To most of them Communism isn't just dead, it was never there.' He paused. 'Schmidt's the same.'

'So what's your interest in him?'

'What he knows.'

'Let me get this straight, you're telling me Schmidt works for you?'

'I suppose so.'

I seem to recall my hands clutching at the thin air, trying to decipher what he was saying.

'He's told us about your visitor in East Berlin – the one who got carted off dead, wearing your jacket. He was definitely liaison between the Stasi and the KGB. But what isn't clear is whether he really knew the identity of Moscow's agent in London.'

'Isn't that why he was killed?'

'Possibly.' Keen grinned. 'Probably.'

'Where does Schmidt come in?'

'We'll use him and then trade him. Like a Monopoly card. Regrettably, we need the Schmidts of this world. His old side doesn't matter any more. But we need to know how the jigsaw was put together, who did what to whom, who owed favours that are still in the bank and can be cashed.' He picked up his teacup but then put it back down. 'You see East Germany was into everything, like a robot gone mad, subverting, penetrating, recording. They were masters at it. Only thing was they didn't know when to stop. Until a few days ago they had files that would fill up headlines around the world for years to come.' He paused. 'But then I'm not telling you anything new, am I?'

'Where are the files now?'

He sighed and ran a hand through his hair. 'Moscow got some of them – the big ones, the ones they wanted. The West Germans got a few. Some were lifted out by the Stasi themselves.'

'Schmidt and his colleagues?'

'Perhaps.'

'Why only perhaps?'

'Put it this way.' Keen stood up and returned to the mantelpiece. 'We're at an early stage of the relationship. Not everyone blurts it all out on the first date.'

'So where is this going?'

'Keen went over to the window and looked out. The rain had ceased for a moment, but the guardians still stood there motionless under their umbrellas.

'Schmidt starts his de-briefings here. A week for the first session, then there'll be others. He's been told we'll set him up with the new Christian Democrats, give him a pedigree, buy him some friends and influence. But we can't keep him here for long, we need him in Berlin.'

'Let me guess why.'

He looked at me as if I were a decent meal gone cold. 'Fenton's in Berlin to offer Schmidt to the Russians. They get him if we get the name of their agent in London. They can even lift him out, but we want the name. End of case. Close the file. New era of trust – that sort of pitch. Anyway Schmidt's the biggest fish in the East German dirt-pond, and they've already been after him.'

'To question him or kill him?'

'Both, I expect.'

'That is nice,' I said.

Keen rolled his eyes. 'I sent Clarky to back him up. He's not best pleased with you, lifting his money and cards.'

'So the little tribe is assembling back in Berlin.'

Keen sniffed as if the smell of his own thoughts were unpleasant to him, 'One of them's bent,' he said simply. 'Fenton's been missing for two days. I don't like what I think it means.'

I must have stayed longer than I thought, for when I left, the sky was a darker grey and the wind had picked up, and the waves had literally parted along the causeway, opening the lifeline to the mainland.

I'd asked him what happened to Kirsch and he hadn't said much. 'Own goal I'm afraid. Fellow that we sent to watch you got worried. Kirsch was in your room and armed. Didn't look good. Anyway,' he sniffed again, 'you should be grateful we keep your best interests at heart.'

'I'm delighted,' I said, still wishing I'd had more of a hand in Kirsch's departure.

Keen stood on the doorstep, the wind dancing again with his hair. He was pushing us all back to Berlin, one by one, suspect by suspect, together in the hothouse-city, playground for every dissident group, terrorist faction and intelligence unit that could afford the rents.

One of our little number had got himself another job without telling us. Someone who didn't just want to give up and go to Moscow. Someone who'd stick it out as long as he could. And only in the final moments would he start to run, killing anyone in his path.

I believed I was facing a gambler who was staking his life against mine.

# THIRTY

'I waited for you,' she said. 'I wondered when you'd come,' she said. 'I missed you.'

And something was wrong, because Cassie didn't give away her words that easily. The thoughts were there, but they were the ones she held dearest and tightest to her, and she rarely gave them expression.

She stood in the doorway in the narrow corridor, and we listened to the Berlin traffic outside and the clumping of new hotel guests on the floors above us.

I'd been back in the city for less than an hour, more worried now than when I'd left.

Cassie led me into her room and I couldn't help wanting to believe her. Affection and kindness are powerful stimulants when you're not used to them – and I kept thinking – don't be nice to me, because I'll break down and get silly and do anything you want.

Only now do I believe that is exactly what she may have wanted.

She made me tell her about Keen. No prompting.

Despite all the training, I am still someone who likes to talk. Divide the world into the tellers and the tight-lipped, and I am in the first camp.

But she made it so easy.

Martin, you were like a stray dog, brought in from the cold and given a feed. And you felt warm and happy and when her hand held yours, and her eyes scooped out your thoughts and read them, then there wasn't much you could do to stop it.

I was reaching for her, reaching back four years to the last time I'd held her – and I don't really want to write it down, because it would lose in the telling, but it was the way I remembered, like the two halves of the world fitting back together.

Cassie didn't test or probe – she knew. We knew. And it was always the first time, each time, long, long after it had been.

Lying next to her, aware that only she mattered.

Holding her, fearing time would return and take her from me.

In that moment, deciding never to let that happen.

She wasn't easy with what we'd done. But to Cassie it was a point in her life that she'd reached and couldn't avoid. It wouldn't colour what had gone before or what came later. Nothing to do with anyone else. Different compartment. Different life.

Much later we went out into the city and the lights that she loved, and watched the Berliners returning to the kinds of homes we didn't have.

I held her hand but there was no sense of possession. You didn't possess Cassie. You shared her – deeply or on the surface, a day, a mood, only ever a part. Don't ask for more. Long ago I had learned her philosophy of freedom.

Make no promises, she once said, because if you are true to yourself they are unnecessary. Seek no guarantees, because words can never make sure. Don't question faith, because it can't withstand it. Demand no commitments, because in that demand lie your own doubt and disbelief.

You would ask her in vain to tell you who she was – because she'd dance away and tell you of others, and make you think it was her.

We passed the half-destroyed, spiky finger of the Memorial Church and Cassie broke away from me and looked up at the jagged edge, with its new concrete supports.

'It's like us,' she told me and laughed her old, infectious laugh. 'You're the old ruin and I'm the support. And together we're a church of memories, moments and times and places that are sacred to us.'

From then on it was our 'Memory Church'. A symbol of what we had given to each other, a faith in what the past had meant, and what the future would bring.

And I am not a person who gets premonitions, I don't have the right antennae, don't lie in bed dreaming and wondering and imagining all the things that might come to me – if only they would.

Yet, I was sure of one thing when I took her to her room and left her on the doorstep and held her for the few moments that she'd let me – sure that by the morning she'd be gone.

## THIRTY-ONE

I forced her door. I'd knocked for at least thirty seconds, and I didn't like what I didn't hear.

But Cassie hadn't been in a hurry. Almost ambled out by the look of it. Clothes folded and put away. She'd hung a suit and jacket in the wardrobe. Showed planning. Showed she'd left of her own free will.

I made my way to Clarky's hotel, on foot across West Berlin, past the Memory Church and all that I stored in it.

Downstairs, Clarky and Iris were having breakfast.

'You made it.' Clarky folded a slice of yellow cheese and stuffed it in his mouth. 'Bit offhand wasn't it, pissing off with our money and all that?'

'Sorry, Clarky.'

'Sorry,' he repeated and looked at Iris. 'He says sorry.'

'Never mind,' said Iris. 'I mean he didn't have much choice, after all.'

They told me a little of their time in Berlin. The

outline, the run-in with the Stasi. But I didn't realize until later, how much they'd held back. I mean, Clarky was never that forthcoming. And I suppose Keen had told him to be careful, same as the rest of us. For none of us knew what would happen.

Iris was talking about the weather, in the way people do, searching for a safe subject when there isn't one, and then she stopped, and both of them sat staring over my shoulder. I turned to see what they were looking at and it was the second unpleasant event of the day.

He stood a few feet from the table, unwilling to get closer, and it was some moments before I recalled who he was. Don't forget, I hadn't seen Christian for years and in those days he'd been arrogant and proud and good-looking and brash – the best and the worst of Germany in one sun-tanned body – and it had all belonged to the Service.

Now he was bruised and cowed and looked away as he greeted me – only I could see the missing teeth.

I beckoned him to the table and he sat down gingerly, as if unsure whether he would infect us – or we him. And the three of us just stayed there all British and embarrassed, no small talk in our heads and enough inhibitions to justify a lifetime of therapy. We told him to help himself to the cold table, but he just waved a hand and sat in the corner, playing underdog. So in the end we gave up and asked him why he'd come.

I could tell immediately it was going to be a long story. Christian's English seemed to have been badly damaged in the beating and he found it hard to follow a clear line of thought.

'*Ja*, Herr Martin. Zo. After so much time to see you here. Ten years is already passing, *Ja*?'

I let him ramble on about his car business, and about Niki, one of his employees, who knew how to handle the female customers, personal service, after-sales, and after-hours too, by all accounts. Good old Niki, I thought, and I was just about to tell Christian to bugger off – when the story improved.

Four days earlier Niki had received an unusual request. Would he sell a car for a week, with no paperwork, no questions asked, and a thousand marks in his pocket? The car would be returned to him in exactly seven days, and the deal would be over. The request came from a lady, who on further enquiry worked in the Soviet embassy. 'Nice lady,' Niki had said. 'Classy. Not the usual stiff in skirts. Wore make-up, combed her hair, washed occasionally. Definitely a cut above the others.'

'But Niki is a good boy,' said Christian, as if in our silence, we had dared to impugn his morals. 'Niki vud not take money, vizout giving something back.'

Niki, it seemed, had decided to take matters

further. In the interests, said Christian, of good client relations, he had offered to take the lady to dinner, offered a nightclub, and then with boundless charm and tasteful sophistication, offered his bed – all offers, we were to understand, had been gratefully accepted.

Christian stopped and examined the three of us through pained eyes. 'I think I eat something after all,' he said.

'Later,' I told him. 'Don't mess about, Christian. Let's have it now.'

He seemed surprised by the sharpness in my voice, but it had the right effect.

'Look, all this happen just two days ago. Lady stays the night, luvvy-duvvy, wonderful time, best since for ever . . . *ja*, OK? This you can imagine. And then she thanks him for the car and says she has to go. "Why you need this car?" Niki asks. "Can't tell you," she replies.' Christian laughed. 'So then Niki take her back to bed and she tells everything.'

I looked at him in disbelief, but a smile had formed on his swollen lips and it was suddenly clear he had begun playing the game again. Christian was still Christian, even without his front teeth. Still the Berlin expert, still the man who'd worked the city for us, all those years ago.

His eyes seemed to have cleared of pain. 'It seems,' he said, 'she was given very precise instructions. That's new. Normally, she says to

Niki, they tell her nothing, trust her with nothing, and can't make up their minds even what to have for lunch. She's East German, she notices these things. OK, so now they tell her to find an ordinary car, ordinary colour, go to the S-Bahn station at Savignyplatz, pick up a man in brown coat, carrying blue file. Take him to Soviet embassy, back door, straight in, then wait, take him back to Western side. Wall is open, traffic is free. No problem. OK?' Christian paused and swallowed, and now he was back in business, running with it, the old Christian alive, focused.

'First time she goes over, no one shows. Second time, he's there. Gets in the car and says nothing. She takes him to the Embassy and waits, but when he comes back, he's not alone. Young Russian diplomat with him. They get in, tell her to drive them to the Wannsee. Nice sunny day. The two of them get out, chat, walk around a bit. She takes the Russian back, and the other guy stays there.'

Christian poured himself a glass of water.

I think I knew what was coming next, but I didn't want to prompt him. Always let them tell it their own way, with their own details and snapshots. Only nudge when you have to.

'Zo, it's like this,' Christian puts down the water. 'Yesterday, Niki puts a device in the car. I had one left from the Americans. Homing thing. Works like dream. And we follow. All the way to Savigny-platz, and then straight to Wannsee. Russian diplomat arrives on foot. Nobody else present.' He licked his lips. 'And this is why I come to you, Herr Martin.'

'Why?'

'Why?' he repeated and shook his head. 'You know I have pair of good field glasses, special. So, yesterday at the lake it was no problem to see both of them. Bright day, good sunlight. And for a while the fellow in the brown coat looked like a stranger. And then I think to myself . . . maybe I seen him before, maybe here in Berlin, maybe that trip to London I did once. And then it comes to me – little older, little less hair, but the walk, always the walk, Herr Martin, this never changes. Fenton.' He drew in his breath. 'Harry Fenton. No doubt about it.'

I told Christian to wait on the street corner and then turned to Clarky.

'Did you know any of this about Fenton?'

He shook his head. 'He was supposed to maintain contact. Tell us his movements, and we'd watch his back. We lost contact two days ago.'

I didn't like that. God knew who Fenton was working for, let alone Christian or anyone else.

I joined Christian on the street.

'Whose side are you on these days?'

'To tell you the truth, Herr Martin, it varies. These are days of, shall we say, private enterprise.'

'You won't survive long, like that.' I said. 'Not in this city.'

'Maybe none of us will.' He shrugged. 'Anyway, Herr Martin,' he glanced up and down the street, 'if I can be of service . . .'

He let the words hang there on the street corner, as if waiting for me to pick them up.

## THIRTY-TWO

I took an hour to think it over, meandering along with the crowds on the Ku-Damm. It was late afternoon and in the East I'd always looked up at that time and watched the sun doing the imposs- ible, heading over the Wall and into the West. And I'd thought, Maybe I'll never get to do that . . .

I phoned Christian back and told him to mount the surveillance from the next morning. Eight sharp. Office hours. I'd be there too.

'This I was expecting, Herr Martin,' he replied sweetly.

And aren't you the bloody clairvoyant, I thought. But I let him have his toothless smile and told him not to be late, and wondered again who he worked for.

You forget how boring it is just watching. After an hour or so it's a real event when a dog cocks its leg against a tree, when a man has a row with his wife – and if you're really lucky, there's a minor car crash just to help the day along.

But no dog was on hand, just the tourists jumping across the border a few times to prove it was now all right, and no one was going to shoot, and what a silly, unnecessary process the whole thing had been for the last thirty years.

At that time Communism only had a few days to run. Once you took away the Wall you could see it for what it really was. It must have been something like the destruction of the Ancient Gods in Rome. When they pulled down the statues, there was nothing left – no myth, no influence, just the gaping memory of wasted time and more important – wasted lives.

I don't know why but I thought of Glick and the others who'd lived in my block – and how they'd so cheerfully joined in the singing of slogans and the slamming of doors. What had happened to them now? Were they lost and broken, or had they simply borrowed another ideology and gone on as before? Maybe they were just like Schmidt. Maybe we all were.

From our position near the Soviet embassy the Brandenburg Gate dominated the skyline, but did nothing for us. We took it in turns to doze, even though we'd all slept the night before. Niki joined us at lunchtime, bringing sandwiches and beer, and that only made it harder to stay awake. Soon it was mid-afternoon, and the car hadn't moved from the Embassy compound and I think we all believed we'd lost the thread.

'Zo, Herr Martin.' Christian sighed and looked at me as if it were my fault.

I got out of the car and stretched my legs and worried about where to go next, where Cassie was, what Fenton thought he was up to. It occurred to me that Keen might not trust Fenton any more than I did, maybe he wasn't sure about Clarky, or me . . . and then deep down inside I saw the beginnings of a question that I didn't even want to ask, and couldn't begin to answer. I had the strong sensation of being pulled in different directions, tripping over shadows and bodies and always in the same tight circle. The same faces. Put them under pressure, I thought, and something would show, somebody would break. I'd see a sign and I'd know.

Beside the gate a tourist bus had drawn up and I could hear an American woman, asking if this was the real Berlin Wall, because it didn't look high enough and she couldn't see any guards.

On other days I'd have laughed. I used to have a good sense of humour . . . oh, a long time ago – before I met Keen, before I got swallowed up by East Germany, and the games became serious.

I stepped off the kerb . . .

'You should take more care, Herr Martin.' Just a moment of shock for I had walked into Christian's car door, and the back was open and we were on the move and suddenly my thoughts were cut in mid-sentence as the vehicle gathered speed.

Niki was in the driver's seat. Christian fiddling

with the homing receiver and the engine under severe pressure. Already we were halfway down Unter den Linden, heading for the Central Committee.

'They're in a hurry, must be about thirty seconds in front of us. Niki, for God's sake . . .'

Niki swerved to avoid a parked truck that he should have seen about an hour earlier. I had the vision of a dark diminutive figure, clinging to an outsize steering wheel. The car was driving Niki.

On our right the television tower came and went, so did the signs for Potsdam and the transit routes to Poland. The rush-hour traffic caught and held us and it didn't look then as though much had changed. The same stinking piles of nuts and bolts that only the Communists ever called cars – the same flat, unemotional faces, sitting detached behind their windscreens. And Christian cursing them all to hell and back again, as Niki suddenly took to the middle lane, revving forward into the oncoming cars.

I closed my eyes, but he must have done something right, for we screeched across the intersection, down into an underpass, skirting the long lines, and Niki seemed to be learning.

The traffic had begun to ease as we moved southeast. And now we could be going anywhere. For the route feeds into the Berliner Ring – once the most heavily guarded road in the world. You never saw it at first glance, but almost the entire stretch was under surveillance – cameras in the trees and bushes, sensors along the road, automatic alarms that could tell them if cars had stopped – and a whole back-up team of helicopters and Stasi troops, just in case some traveller was stupid enough to veer off the main road and stop for a sandwich.

Christian was shaking his head and pressing switches on the receiver, and we jumped a set of lights. A level crossing appeared in the distance. Cars stopped by the barrier. An endless goods train, trundling about its business.

'Turn for Christ's sake.' Christian was grabbing the wheel, almost out of Niki's grasp.

'*Himmel, Arsch und Zwirn*,' Niki, pushing him away, invoked that most German of all expletives – heaven, arse and dwarf. And I couldn't help thinking we'd probably been away from this side of the business a little too long, our nerves a little too shaky, our edges blunted.

We were driving back into the city. Niki took some of the weight off his right foot and the smell of burning rubber became less pungent. If this were a game ... I thought, for we were fast approaching the Schönhauser Allee and the home ground I had fervently hoped not to see again. And there were all the landmarks, the newspaper kiosk, a few of the old faces, a street-cleaner.

We turned left off the main road and into the avenues with the once-fine mansions of the Prenzlauer Berg. The whole area seemed asleep in the late-afternoon sunshine. Asleep or dying.

For the first time I could see it as a stranger – the grey, stone houses in the straightest of lines, with figures and etchings and faces, now cracked and grimy. A cobbled street with so many cobbles missing, bullet holes in the walls – the heart of a city that was broken and never mended.

Only one building they repaired. Five storeys of red brick – in among all that grey.

I didn't know then why we pulled up there, but even from the car I could make out the black, wrought-iron railings that carried the Star of David, the courtyard beyond, darkened by trees.

Niki switched off the engine and he was pointing down the street to the old water-tower, now converted into flats, and I assumed he had located his car.

They both looked at me, waiting for a sign or an instruction. I wound down the window. It was quiet, but there was no sense of peace. I waited a minute. Two. But nobody came. On the street the wind was turning the leaves in circles like the patterns of history. A dog began barking incessantly. Across the road the shops were shuttered, perhaps in expectation of better times. And in a window high above the street a child's pink dress was hanging for all the world to admire.

Rykestrasse – number 53. Site of the Jewish synagogue.

Christian reached under his seat, brought out an automatic and checked there was a bullet in the breach.

## THIRTY-THREE

Why did I feel no sense of urgency? Christian and
Niki stood each side of me like bloodhounds, waiting to slip their chains. But to me the stillness of the
courtyard was suffocating – the long shadows,
the violent history, the knowledge that people had
prayed on this small square of ground in fear of
their lives.

To lead someone here was to bring them to a
place of sadness and suffering.

I looked up to the windows, but the reflection of
light on glass prevented me seeing through them.
Only that didn't matter. Some things you take on
trust – even danger and evil. You don't have to see
them to know they're there.

Christian tried the door to the synagogue. It was
locked, and apart from us and the trees and a row
of giant dustbins, there was nothing in sight.

'We take a look around,' said Niki, and from the
way he was holding his jacket, I assumed he too
was armed.

They left me standing there, worrying about the
place and the reasons we'd been brought to it, and

something seemed to nag at my memory. An image or some words or a fact I had seen once, such a long time ago.

I sat on the steps of the synagogue and looked up into the trees, and then I could see a photo in a black cardboard file, and Kirsch's face in my office and the re-touched picture of the general secretary on the wall.

One of the worst memories from the little pile I'd assembled in East Berlin.

I think I knew then what it had all been about.

'Jews, Herr Martin,' Kirsch had said to me that bitter-cold afternoon, my first December in Berlin, my first full day at Stasi headquarters. I had been staring out of the window at the shops – full of what the East always called '*Jahresendzeitfiguren*' – end of the year figures – the closest they were allowed to Father Christmas.

'Jews,' he repeated, but he'd already got my attention. Whichever side of the Wall you lived – the word invoked a half century of guilty consciences.

'What about them, Herr Kirsch?'

'What is your feeling about them?' he countered.

'I have no feeling.'

He seemed to consider that for a moment. 'I also have no feelings, Herr Martin. As you know religious tolerance is assured by the constitution of the German Democratic Republic. For this reason we have protected the Jewish cemetery and rebuilt the synagogue.'

'A fine achievement, Herr Kirsch.'

'Exactly.'

He stood a long time before producing the file from behind his back. And I remember feeling my first twinge of anticipation since arriving in the city. For six months I had done nothing but tell and re-tell my half-invented story. Why I'd come over, what had converted me, who I really was and where I'd really been – in offices, in restaurants, in country houses with people I'd never seen and never would see.

And now I had a desk in Stasi headquarters and I was about to find out why.

Kirsch removed a single sheet of paper from the file and handed it to me. It was thin and close-typed and carried the stamp '*streng-geheim*' – top secret.

'There are no copies, Herr Martin.' He leaned forward. 'And there will be no copies, *ja*?'

I remembered thinking I had better take in every word, because there would be no second chance, no follow-up. And in a day or a week or a year, it would cease to exist.

According to the account the East German leader had just returned from Moscow. As usual it was a toss-up who had been more sick – he or his Russian counterpart; or maybe it was the awful food getting to both of them. At any rate, as soon as the dinner ended the Soviet leader steered his guest into an ante-room, clutching a bottle of brandy and wearing the first glint of the day in his eyes.

Not so his guest. Armed with all the piousness of a true bigot, the East German declined such decadent excess and contented himself with coffee, mineral water and the usual helping of Marxist clichés. Somewhere in the middle of all this fun, the Soviet leader must have mumbled a phrase or two about the Americans, for his guest immediately adjusted his hearing aid and began trying to locate his memory.

Despite all appearances, he was told, the Kremlin could from time to time, negotiate with the Americans. They were tough, they were ruthless – but they understood the ways of the world.

'*S nimi mozhno vyesti dyelo*,' the old Russian had said. 'You can do business with them.'

'Such as?'

The Russian tapped his nose. 'New arrangements, my friend, accommodations in Europe and the Far East, Central America, the Persian Gulf. Yalta was many years ago. Time to move on.'

'I should be interested to hear of such things,' the East German leader shifted uneasily in the armchair.

'In good time, my friend. In good time. We have an excellent young ambassador in your city, who has undertaken some of the contacts – a Jew by the way.' The Russian looked hard at his guest.

'I didn't know that.'

They surveyed each other in silence.

'Not of course that it makes any difference.'

'Indeed.'

I remember looking up at Kirsch at this point and shaking my head in disbelief. 'Where did you get all this?' I asked.

'The interpreter,' he replied. 'We supply them to the Central Committee and all senior officials.'

I went back to my reading, but the text petered out. A few phrases about the East German's deteriorating temper, how he'd blamed everyone for losing his medicine and then found it later in his coat pocket, a row with his son on the telephone . . .

Reluctantly I handed the paper back to Kirsch. It was the best reading I'd had for years.

'Zo, Herr Martin,' Kirsch produced a handkerchief and wiped his oily forehead. 'Our task now is to find out what the Soviet ambassador is doing, who he meets, who he talks to, who he sleeps with – and what is his deal with the Americans.' He paused. 'Your task.'

'Shouldn't take long,' I said smiling.

Kirsch took the file and walked out. To me his expression of annoyance and bewilderment was reward enough.

It marked, though, my baptism into the Stasi. From that day on I had my own *Abteilung*, with my own little staff of watchers and researchers and a mythical, miserly budget that generated far more paper than money, and far more inquiries than the entire investigation.

And yet we went at it, with true, socialist enthusiasm, following the Soviet ambassador almost to the lavatory – which we succeeded eventually in bugging – from house to car to reception to weekend retreat, and once even to the Jewish cemetery, for no good reason that we could discover.

But here was a man apparently devoid of sins, major or minor – no mistresses, animals or little boys. No gambling or over-spending. No laughs nor tears – and no American contact. He was, in short, one of the most boring men I had ever known.

But how to tell Kirsch? My lack of results seemed only to provoke greater anxiety and instructions to redouble my efforts. Kirsch implied he was being leaned on from a great height and it didn't take much imagination to see who was leaning.

More watchers and researchers arrived and another room was added to my empire; and of course there were hints that if I cracked this one, I'd be in the fast lane for good, and if I didn't I wouldn't be in any lane at all.

A month went by and I had a stack of photographs of the ambassador from all angles. I had copies of his most sensitive correspondence with Moscow. What's more I had accounts of a whole series of ludicrous attempts to seduce him, suborn him, drug him and offer him dollars for roubles. All had failed.

In my office I caught the staff talking about that 'cunning Jew', the 'Jew from Moscow', 'Moscow's Jew boy' and I began to realize their stake in this.

What I didn't realize was how quickly the wind could change direction – Kirsch striding into the office one morning, hauling me to an ante-room announcing with total lack of ceremony or tact or charm that the entire operation was terminated.

'I don't understand,' I told him.

'That is of little consequence.'

'On the contrary,' I interrupted. 'If you expect me to work effectively . . .'

'I expect you to carry out orders. Have the paperwork assembled and delivered to my office. You are to cease surveillance immediately.'

It would be wrong to say my pride had been slighted. But I walked away from Kirsch feeling profoundly uneasy. I had failed my first test, not because of my incompetence, but because the test had produced the wrong results. The Soviet ambassador was clean. At least he was clean now. And that was the last thing Berlin wanted to hear.

I was relieved of most of my staff and relegated back to the room overlooking the main street. No documents arrived in the internal mail. I began to turn up for work at eight and leave at four and do nothing in between.

I remember standing at the bus stop, trying to hide from the wind behind a fat lady with baskets, when I felt a tug at my arm. Hilde, my secretary, a thin, spindly twenty-year-old, who had once held ambitions to be a swimmer, beckoned me to follow her and began walking away down the street.

'What is this about, Hilde?' I asked after about thirty yards.

'Please keep walking, Herr Martin, there are cameras on this street and we don't wish to attract attention, *nicht wahr*?'

No argument from me on that front, but it would have been hard to pick us out. It was already dark, and the streetlamps were dim and the rush-hour traffic was building steadily.

Hilde was cold, muffled up to the neck, her nose streaming. 'It's about the Jewish ambassador . . .'

'You mean the Soviet ambassador?'

'*Ja*, of course.' A glint of incomprehension flashed across her face. 'Today I met a friend of mine from a different section.'

'Which one?'

'Section 16. It seems our report has gone to them, Herr Martin. I thought you would wish to know.'

I don't remember saying anything for a while. I recall the feeling of nausea spreading outwards and upwards from my stomach, rising in my throat. Section 16 was active measures – robbery, assassination – all the rough stuff that the Stasi used and exported to such good effect.

Hilde must have disappeared in the crowd, for I went home alone and sat for hours in the kitchen, unable to suppress my fear. If the papers had gone to Section 16 that could only mean they were preparing for a hit. They had no proof against the ambassador, no evidence, just a throwaway line from a drunk Party leader in Moscow. And because of that they would liquidate him. Out of frustration, out of paranoia, out of a desire to teach the Russians not to be clever on East German soil.

Sometime that night I recall getting out of bed, dressing and walking the streets, wondering what to do. An innocent man was about to be killed. Didn't that surmount all other considerations? Could I approach Kirsch? Would that finish whatever career I still had left? Who could I ask?

In a ghastly way, I suppose I grew up that night. For as the dawn appeared way off over Poland, I realized that I was divorced once and for all from normal human values. I was on an island without morality, and without considerations of right and wrong. My duty was solely to survive for the day when I might be needed. I had finally crossed into a no-man's land more terrifying than the one East Germany had constructed – with its mines and scatter guns and barbed wire. I would let a man die, knowing he was innocent of all crimes.

That morning I went to work, trying to disconnect my thoughts. I had washed my hands and was simply waiting for the consequences. They weren't long in coming.

Two days later, Kirsch summoned me to his office.

'Congratulations are in order, I believe, Herr Martin,' he said, patting my shoulder awkwardly and with far too much force.

'Why is that?'

'The matter of the Jewish ambassador has been satisfactorily settled.' He sat at his desk and put his feet on it. 'It appears that once your surveillance was lifted, he resumed his illegal activities – that is to say his contacts with American agents. One of our other sections picked him up by chance at a meeting at the Jewish synagogue, but he resisted, drew a weapon and was shot by our security forces. A most unpleasant incident, and particularly embarrassing to our Soviet comrades.'

'Indeed.' I couldn't think of anything else to say.

'However,' Kirsch continued, 'it has been recognized that this matter could not have been handled without the painstaking research completed by your department.'

'But my research showed no irregularities . . .'

'On the contrary, Herr Martin, it showed a man, who was clearly too perfect to be real. It showed there was a need for other measures.' He stood up to signify the end of the meeting. 'You have done yourself much good, Herr Martin.'

I was about to leave when a thought struck me

and I turned back to Kirsch. 'What would have happened if he had really not been guilty?'

Kirsch grinned. 'We would have made him guilty.'

On reflection, it was one of the few honest answers I received in the East.

So that was how I remembered the Jewish synagogue in Rykestrasse and why it all seemed so familiar that afternoon, with the crazy car chase through East Berlin, with Niki and Christian champing for action.

I got up off the steps of the building and there was one last memory of the Soviet ambassador that I didn't want to explore again . . . the way he'd been found, over there in the corner . . .

I looked at the ground and started walking, trying to believe that history never repeats itself, that lightning never strikes twice in the same place, repeating the clichés over to myself for comfort.

Across the cemented stone towards those high, rubbish containers and I started to feel that cold finger of intuition, even before I saw the hand lying there half-obscured by a cardboard box. Two more strides and I was tearing away the filth and the paper, seeing the clothes and the figure face down on that concrete, unmoving, unfeeling – just so much the package of a human life, now finished and discarded.

Four years since I'd seen you, Harry Fenton . . .

whoever you were, whatever you were . . .

But he wasn't alone. A foot away, lying on his arm, was the body of a man in a cheap, grey suit. Cheap because it was frayed at the sleeves, and even at that angle would never have buttoned across his stomach. Dead because . . . And I didn't need to look in his pockets to know he was Soviet. The jacket label was in Cyrillic script, the pale cheeks coloured by a Moscow diet . . .

So this had been what they were tidying up. The operation that the old Soviet leader had half confided to his East German counterpart all those years ago. True after all. More true than I had ever imagined. A superpower deal, born of the frustrations and stalemates of the Cold War. A deal re-dividing the spheres of influence. Europe to the Russians, the Pacific to the Americans. This was how the leaders did their duty and earned their money. A grand scheme, planned, perhaps even implemented, now to be buried with no honours of any kind.

I stood there trying to work out who would have killed Fenton and the Russian. Not his own side. Not ours either. And then it seemed, like so many complicated things, so simple and logical.

The two of them under surveillance by the Stasi, the Stasi settling their old scores with Moscow and all who dealt with her.

Natural justice, they would have called it. Back to the Jewish synagogue. The circle complete.

And then I turned round, somehow unsurprised to see Cassie standing there in a white mac and black shoes, looking beyond me, somewhere towards a different world, transfixed, immovable, lost deep inside herself in loneliness and grief.

## THIRTY-FOUR

And so Keen came to Berlin.

I met him on the S-Bahn, clattering and bumping from West to East with the rain pouring down the windows and the passengers sitting cold and dour.

'Miserable buggers,' he observed. 'You'd think they'd be a little happier now the bloody Wall's down.'

Keen could always be relied on to misjudge the mood. As for me – I could understand the sadness. Everything had changed, but nothing had changed. The East Berliners still went home to their dilapidated, second-class city. So what if they'd had a Coke and a hamburger in the West? It was still a foreign land – and to them, perhaps, it always would be.

'The fellow with Fenton was from the Soviet embassy,' he said abruptly.

'So they were going to trade with us after all?'

Keen didn't answer. The train jerked suddenly over the points and I had to struggle to keep my balance.

'How is she now?' he asked and then added with an effort, 'Cassie.'

'Much as expected,' I replied, playing the game. I wasn't going to discuss feelings with Keen, wasn't going to tell him, how she had sat up stiff and silent through the night, unable to talk or cry. How the tears had come finally with the daylight, as she wept her husband from her system.

'Even with all his craziness, he was a good person,' she had said at one point.

'I know,' I replied, and felt ashamed because I had such a different opinion of him.

We pulled into Bellevue Station and beyond the river and the trees you could see the huge Charité hospital, over in the East.

Keen opened the carriage doors and stepped on to the platform. 'This is as far as I go,' he announced. And we stood there watching the little red train move away into a tight curve, with the Reichstag in full view and beyond it – the ploughed death strip, the watch towers, the elaborate paraphernalia of repression.

I couldn't help looking and wondering if it had ever really existed. How could the rest of the world have accepted it, visited it, played with it? Why did they let it happen?

Keen too, was staring into the East but he wouldn't go there. Not until he was sure it was all over, the dragons dismembered, the tortured souls released, justice done. And when would that be?

We began walking slowly towards the exit.

'Did your friend say where she'd been for the last few days?'

Odd that he couldn't bring himself to use her name.

'Not really. She'd been looking for Fenton through American channels. Apparently, when it was clear he'd gone missing, the Agency made it an official inquiry.'

'I know.'

'Yes of course. You would.'

We left the station and headed out into the rain towards the old Reichstag and the holes in the Wall.

To the left the Soviet War Memorial, with its obsolete tanks and expressionless soldier-guards in capes.

'I can't help feeling this is about more than a name,' Keen said. 'Have you ever thought Moscow may be trying to tell us something completely different.'

'What makes you say that?'

He didn't answer for a moment. Instead he stopped and looked back at the Memorial as if the key to it all lay there. 'It's just that I can't find any other explanation for why you're still alive,' he said. 'For a traitor who's killed so often, he seems remarkably unwilling to finish the job.'

By this time we were hard up against the Wall. And

even in the dreadful weather dozens of people stood around, talking and arguing, trying to make sense of it, before the bulldozers pulled it down. You could tell they were from both the Eastern and Western halves of the city – spontaneous gatherings of people who could never in their short lives have met like this, because their politicians didn't let them. Truly, I thought, the world had little to be proud of.

Above the Brandenburg Gate a helicopter began hovering at about five hundred feet – probably a television team. Keen pulled up his collar and looked at the ground.

'We have to make contact with the Russians.'

He kicked a stone and watched it slither towards the Wall. 'If the things you heard about in the Stasi are true, we might be looking at deals and decisions that could destabilize Europe for years to come . . .'

'But the Russians are a spent force. They've just lost Eastern Europe. They're tearing themselves to pieces . . .'

'It's not just the Russians, is it?' Finally Keen looked up at me. The helicopter had gone. The rain had eased. 'There were two superpowers, remember? It could be the Americans as well.'

She was packing when I knocked at the door.

'Cassie?'

'They've asked me to go back to the States.'

Different Cassie now, I thought. The face looked so thin and tight. There was little strength left. The voice and the composure could crack at any time.

'I'm taking Harry back with me. He'll be buried in Washington. Do you know, there isn't a single member of his family . . .' She stopped and sat down on the bed. A porter knocked at the door and she beckoned him in to take the suitcases.

'I'll come to see you when I'm finished here.'

She shook her head. 'I can't even think about that right now. I have to deal with all this, with Harry, with a lot of questions and a lot of issues I don't even understand. I won't be a very good person to talk to for some time.'

'Yes, you will.'

I held her head on my shoulder, and felt the rough, thick hair on my cheek. The silence was full of all the things I wanted her to say – and all the things she wouldn't. Her sadness seemed to fill the room, and even after she'd got up and left, and I heard the car drive away and the dark came down over the city, I could still feel it in the stillness and emptiness that she'd left behind.

## THIRTY-FIVE

They flew Schmidt to Germany in a military jump jet – a sensation, described as something between a car crash and an orgasm; and for Schmidt I hoped fervently it was the former.

Yet, Keen told me he looked disgustingly at ease, clambering out of the cockpit and into the field, just north of Berlin's British Sector, where they had chosen the site for the landing.

I suppose they also wanted to test whether East Germany still possessed Air Defences, so it was probably safe to assume they didn't.

We had 'a little briefing' in Keen's hotel room. Clarky and me and Iris – yes, Iris too, because as Keen put it, 'What the hell, he's bound to tell her everything anyway.' And it was funny how all the niceties were observed – coffee in a huge thermos jug, sandwiches – 'Anyone fancy a cake?' – Iris annoying Keen intensely by saying 'Yes,' and then delaying the discussion till it arrived.

'Right,' says Keen, and Clarky starts coughing uncontrollably for several minutes. 'As you know I've brought Schmidt back with me.' And we all looked round embarrassed and awkward, for there we were to discuss the betrayal and death of a man who, loathsome as he was, had been careless enough to trust us.

'Don't you think it's just a little too dishonourable to throw Schmidt to the Russians, after promising him all the things you presumably *have* promised him?' Clarky voicing the pro-forma reservations.

'No choice,' announces Keen intolerantly. 'We have nothing else to bargain with . . . Besides he wasn't much of a saint in the old GDR . . . was he?'

We all sat back and looked unhappily at each other. I wished it was a game, where I could put down my cards, get up from the table and walk away. But I knew I still hadn't paid my debts.

If anyone had recorded the minutes of this bizarre meeting, it would probably have read like this: Chairman's appreciation and words of welcome. Discussion about how best to eliminate subject concerned. Agreement that Clarky would handle new approach to Soviet embassy. Aforementioned Clarky confirmed he knew a Berlin man from the old days who would 'realize the score', 'see where I was coming from', 'be sensible about it'.

Only there were no minutes. No sense of formality. Just a little group of rather nervous, and incompetent individuals playing games that should long ago have been restricted to boards and counters, but for reasons they had forgotten, had somehow translated into real life.

As for Schmidt – he was in a safe place.

'How safe?' asked Clarky.

'Christian's got him,' Keen said and raised his eyebrows as if he wasn't any happier about it than we were. 'Christian's got him.'

I waited for Clarky and Iris to leave before saying what I thought.

'You don't have clearance for any of this, do you?'

'What makes you say that?'

'You wouldn't be using Christian if you did. It would be the full back-up team from London, all those nice young men with the coloured umbrellas, proper safe house. But you're out there on your own this time, aren't you?'

Keen opened his mouth to say something, then stopped and looked round the room. 'Listen, Martin, I don't have clearance to go out and buy envelopes, these days.' He walked over to the window. 'They don't want this sort of thing any more – the politicians. No votes in it. Can't have people wandering round Europe, putting muddy feet on all the conference tables. Not when they're so busy signing names on pieces of paper and calling them treaties.' He sat down again at the table and blew out his cheeks. 'Bury it, they said, the whole lot. Never happened – any of it. What matters is now. The new order, new people, new countries. If you can't cope with that – find someone who can.'

'Are they right?'

Keen looked at me perplexed and angry. 'Of course they are. But I can't let it go at that. Spent too many years tracking these lying, twisting bastards . . .'

'Till you became one yourself.'

Keen looked at me and giggled for the first time since arriving in Berlin. 'You wouldn't have said that, four years ago.'

'But I thought it,' I said, holding his eyes, refusing to let them divert.

'I suppose you did.'

'I still do.'

And then there was a moment that I've thought about for a long time since. A moment when I saw Keen look dejected and broken, believing as he surely did, that I would walk out, and abandon the operation, and he'd never find out what had happened.

I suppose there comes a time for many of us – when we stare deep into our own lives and realize we've failed, a point when the illusions and the comfort they've given us melt away. Maybe the young can pick themselves up and find other roads. But not Keen. He didn't know any other roads and was too tired and discouraged to go exploring.

I hope I never feel the way he looked, on that afternoon in Berlin, sitting in his bedroom in his old tweeds, with the grey hair sticking out in all directions, surrounded by dirty coffee cups and cake crumbs. I don't want to look back and think of a whole collection of 'could-have-beens' and 'might-have-beens' and 'if-onlys'. I don't want to remember a time when I gave up the dream or the ambition or the purpose. And I won't.

So it was as much for me as for him that I told him I'd see it through. And then it would be over. He could spend his days chewing grass for all I cared, but I'd be on my way – and I knew where that was, and from the light in his eye, so did he.

'I hope you make it,' he said, 'both of you,' reminding me once again, that in seeing out his plan, neither of us might survive beyond it.

## THIRTY-SIX

Schmidt had apparently become sullen and bad-
tempered and I felt good about that. It would have
been awful to sell him out if he'd been humble and
grateful and full of the milk of human kindness.
But then, I suppose, he wouldn't have been
Schmidt.

Keen took me to Christian's house to relieve him.
His nerves were in poor shape.

'This man, Herr Martin, he is truly a bastard, one
of the worst, I tell you. You should have nothing to
do with him.'

'Why?'

'Always he is complaining and wanting something. A drink, a smoke, then he wants to crap for
an hour. When he comes back his coffee is cold.
"Was never like this in the DDR," he says. So I have
to fetch new pot. I am like nursemaid.'

I went into the hall, and was struck by the bare
white walls and the bare wooden floor. Schmidt
wasn't getting the luxury package – not by any
means.

Keen had briefed me on what to say. 'Tell him

the same thing I did. He's been brought to Berlin so we can check some of the details of his story.'

'Sounds plausible enough.'

'Well, it won't to Schmidt.'

'Why not?'

Keen gave his familiar giggle. 'Because he hasn't told us anything worth checking. He'll know that.'

Schmidt got up from the sofa as I came in, and I could read the relief in his eyes – not that I was a friend or an ally. But he would be recalling the time we'd met in that bunker in Potsdam, where it was he who'd been in charge, he who'd done the manipulating – just as he would seek to do it again.

'Herr Martin, good to see you again.' One hand went for mine, the other clasped my shoulder and I could smell alcohol on his breath. For one ludicrous moment it seemed he wanted to dance.

'I trust you're being well treated?' I asked, pulling away from him.

'Regrettably not.' He reclaimed the sofa, letting his bulk fill it. 'I did not wish to return to Berlin until proper preparations . . .'

'You mean, without a bunch of Stasi to protect you.'

Schmidt crossed his legs, resting a hand on his ankle.

'Herr Martin, let me explain some things to you. When you worked for us, this was a sham, *Ja*? This is now clear. You were a long-term sleeper. Only, of course, the one problem was with the wake-up call – it never came.' He chuckled and I watched him, feeling the nausea rise in my throat.

'To me, Herr Martin, it was also a sham. Communism, in my case, had many benefits. I already owned a Mercedes, a boat, cameras and watches . . .' he pointed to a gold slab on his wrist. 'I did not have to wait fifteen years for a two-room flat. But to me, it was simply like any other society with those who win and those who lose. The system was an experiment. Some wanted it, others didn't. Perhaps we had to go through this to find the way forward.' He was sweating freely just as he had in the bunker. 'I tell you this, Herr Martin, because I wanted to return – not with Stasi to protect me, as you say, but to play a part in the political life of the new Germany. This was what I understood also to be the interest of the British Service. In return for information on my past life, they would help me in my future life. There were to be plans and detailed preparations and now I am brought here . . .'

'What qualifies you to play a part?'

'The question is stupid, Herr Martin. All this talk of a new society, why? Are the people on the streets of Berlin different from yesterday? Do they live different lives, have different ambitions?'

He looked at me as if expecting an answer.

'Of course they do not. The question then is how they are to be governed. I was able to play a part before. Methods, of course, must change, but principles must stay the same – the wise channel-ling of human energies . . .'

'Wise, Herr Schmidt?'

'We made mistakes. But we learn. After all, we are Germans.'

He wasn't much of an orator, but there was something insidiously convincing about him. On any level, Schmidt was a persuader. But you couldn't forget that wherever there was a Schmidt, there would always be a Kirsch, the made-to-order thug, hiding behind him, then coming out in the darkness to clear the path ahead of him. At least, though, Kirsch was dead, and for the same good reasons, it didn't seem to matter any more what happened to Schmidt.

'Out of interest, Herr Martin,' he went over to a cupboard on the wall and removed a bottle of whisky, 'what is the exact reason for my visit to Berlin?'

'All in good time,' I told him. 'One really shouldn't hurry these things.'

I had dinner that night with Keen, though I'd rather have had it alone. It was a Sunday night and I've never coped well with them. A hang-over from childhood – that feeling of having to return to school the next day, with the homework only half done, and a seemingly endless stream of tests and classes and competitions ahead.

My father would come into my bedroom around

eight o'clock and give me my pocket money – but only if I told him how I'd spent the last lot. So on Sundays I had the additional task of making up accounts for the week before, and trying to find excuses for having lost the money, eaten it, or gambled it away.

As I grew older, it felt as if a black dog would enter the house on those Sunday evenings, imbuing the place with a deep sense of melancholy. We would always watch a bit of television, *Danger Man* or *The Saint* or some such other pick-me-up, but the dog would be there at the end of it, watching me with its dark brown eyes. I would pack my satchel and clean my shoes and lie in bed, reciting the poems or psalms to be tested the next day, and I would feel that dog lying across my feet like a dead weight. It was as if he were reminding me for just that one night that the world could be a sad and lonely place to visit, and he knew it because he'd been there.

Each Sunday night in East Berlin the black dog had visited – and now he was there again as I finished dinner with Keen.

'I'm quite glad we're trading Schmidt in.' He pushed away his plate and reached for the wine bottle. 'From what I hear the Bonn government is handing out pardons to the Stasi people as fast as they can be printed.'

'Schmidt told me as much in East Berlin, but I

didn't really believe him. He said they wouldn't go in for witch-hunts.'

Keen sneered. 'Of course they wouldn't. They haven't settled accounts with the last lot from 1945. Now they'll be even less inclined. Look at it this way. They want to unify the country, heal the wounds. A whole load of trials and investigations would only have the opposite effect. Besides if you start digging into who did what in East Germany, where do you stop? There aren't too many clear consciences over there. And in a way that was what the Communists always hoped for. If everyone was involved in the police state, then no one would want to get rid of it.'

'Only that didn't work either.'

Keen shook his head. 'If the East Germans couldn't make Communism work, then no one could. They gave it the best shot, they were the most efficient . . . but I think in the end, the people themselves became so revolted, they wouldn't tolerate it any longer.'

He paid the bill and stood up. The restaurant had emptied. The lights had dimmed and the waiters seemed glad to see us go.

'We don't have long to settle this thing,' he said as we stood outside. 'If we don't move fast, someone, whoever it is, will bury the information for good.'

Ironically Christian's house was only fifty feet from

the Wall. It was in a long line of modern chalet-style buildings to the north of the British sector, close to open country.

A light was on downstairs and another on the second floor.

'Everything all right?' Christian's face appeared at the front door and he eased it open.

In the kitchen sat Niki, two or three cans of beer, the air full of tobacco smoke.

'He's gone to bed.' Christian said. 'The shit tried to use the telephone.'

'Did you ask him who he was calling?'

'I hit him instead, Herr Martin. There was no point asking.'

We sat disconsolately at the table. 'But there is good news, also.' Christian raised his glass. 'Clarky called. The meeting is fixed. Eleven tomorrow night.'

No one said anything. Someone nudged my foot under the table. If you'd asked me, I would have said it was a black dog.

## THIRTY-SEVEN

After four dead years in East Berlin I knew all about killing time. And yet with a free day there, it was surprising, even to me, how little I wanted to visit. No old girlfriends, no confidants, no churches or museums. No streets with pleasing associations. No echoes worth recalling. I had shaken myself free of all the ties that might once have held me. Now at last, I could dislike it for what it was.

For a while, though, I wandered across the Alexanderplatz settling a ghost or two of my own. My mother's visit – that half day, half a lifetime ago, which had hurt us both so indelibly. Why had I let her go without telling her the truth? Could I not have put her mind to rest? In the grand scheme of things, it would surely have cost so little and meant so much.

She had walked away that afternoon, a little wisp of a thing, so fearful of the East, and even now I can hear those tears and feel them. And long after she had cried herself dry, the hurt would have gone on stabbing at her beliefs and values.

Of course, I could always blame Keen. But then

no one had forced me to follow his instructions, no one forced me to go to Berlin. I simply ran out of options. And when that happened, as it once did to so many misfits, criminals, homosexuals and idealists, you simply went East. God alone knows where you go these days!

I couldn't help finding my way to the Normannenstrasse and contemplating the weird kinds of creatures that had come to earth there.

Hilde, my first secretary – hadn't lasted long. I caught her going through my briefcase, the day after I'd bought it. She was either putting something in or taking something out, and her excuse about looking for a pen didn't seem that imaginative. So after many written applications and interviews Kirsch finally removed her.

Then there was Frau Hagen, always loud and over-cheerful. Sanger, my researcher cum eavesdropper, suggested she was probably 'getting plenty' and since he wasn't, set about trying to share in the fun. I discovered them kissing in the corner of my office, when they thought I'd left for lunch. So Sanger must have had something to offer.

Finally, there came to me a spiky-haired, angular young creature from New York – a twenty-four-year-old lady graduate, who had begun deciding she was a Communist, at about the same time the rest of the world was deciding it wasn't.

She had flown to Berlin, thrown her US passport

into the River Spree and demanded political asylum at Checkpoint Charlie. The guards were delighted, and so were the Stasi. She was a propaganda coup, just when they needed one.

I asked her once why she had come over – what I actually asked was why the 'fucking hell' she'd come over, because by that time I wasn't as discreet as I had been, and because the girl seemed otherwise completely normal.

She'd worked it all out, she said. The balance of power, the way it had shifted, what needed to be done. All over the world, she said, the right wing was celebrating and the left wing was dead. That couldn't be good. Every system needed an opposition. So she'd come to the East to do what she could to help.

I didn't laugh at her. After my years in the Stasi, I'd heard even more ludicrous stories than that. And besides you can't often look for a reasonable motive in a human being.

So she'd joined the team and with the benefit of her fluent Russian and Polish, helped us spy on East Germany's fraternal allies – you know, the Bulgarians and Russians and Poles, the ones to whom they always declared undying love and unity of purpose. And we bugged their embassies, played games with their secret services, and warned them off if they became too cheeky.

My department, it was. Mine. And now when I looked up to the second-storey window above the shops, the blinds had been pulled down the same as in all the other offices. And someone would be going through the files, and like me would conclude that the whole thing had been an almighty waste of money.

I didn't want to stand around too long. Those kinds of thoughts aren't the most productive, and I needed diversion – rather than a day spent peering into my own navel.

But there was one final pilgrimage and then I wouldn't come back – ever. I promised myself that. I'd shake off East Berlin for good, like so much dust on my collar. I'd go to America and visit Cassie . . . and then? And then there was a big full stop, and I couldn't think further than that, couldn't see the sentence beyond.

I took the U-Bahn and the bus to the Schönhauser Allee, determined to enjoy that afternoon, walking past the newspaper kiosk, noticing that the old crone inside was eyeing me all the way. Who was I? she'd be wondering. One of the old lot, or the new lot? Had I somehow denounced her? Was I going to?

It was getting on for five o'clock and the street was filling up and I knew Glick would be on his way home. I sat on the bench and waited, trying to recall the number of times I had walked this way, forgetting who I really was, immersed in the details of the department, the eccentricities of the staff, what kind of dinner I'd cook – the day-to-day and the mundane.

The little boy had stopped on the corner to blow his nose, and my eyes must have followed him for at least a minute, before I realized he was one of the Glick children, his younger brother close behind him. Only ten days since I'd seen them, and yet they looked so different. The older boy was swinging a bag of fruit, a Western carrier bag, he was in a hurry, he was wearing new shoes. Gradually piece by piece I observed this new child phenomenon. East Berlin boy had been over to the West, and was fast becoming West Berlin boy. Soon he'd be chewing gum and buying nudie magazines – and then the GDR would have lost him for good.

I let them go into the block and waited five or ten minutes before following.

It was hard to know what to expect, knocking at that door, hoping at least to surprise them and shake them, and yet find out what they were doing. But it was I who took a step back, as the balding, apologetic figure of Herr Glick, ambled into view wearing one of *my* old cardigans. Mine!

We both stood, with that kind of breathless silence, as if winded by a punch in the stomach. Glick tried speaking only the words wouldn't come.

'Herr Martin,' he managed finally, and then he went red as he looked down at the cardigan and back at me, his hands spreading out in a gesture of defencelessness. 'Herr Martin, it was lying in the rubbish bin . . . I didn't know . . . I . . .'

'Think nothing of it, Glick,' I said luxuriating in his embarrassment. 'I threw it away myself before leaving.' I looked past him into the flat and then out again to the hall. He got the message stepping backwards to usher me in, fumbling with his sweaty hands.

'Anneliese,' he called out. 'It's Herr Martin. He's back. He's . . .'

But Frau Glick was already emerging through the sitting-room door, closing it firmly behind her, a furtive, mousy little thing, putting all her teeth on show as she tried to smile. Suddenly the tiny hall was crowded.

'Herr Martin,' she simpered, 'what a charming surprise.'

'You too,' I breathed. 'How are the boys?'

'You know how it is, Herr Martin. They seem to have colds most of the time. I've tried herbal remedies because we couldn't afford . . .' she broke off. Glick was gesturing wildly, trying to imitate a teapot. It was all I could do to keep from laughing.

Frau Glick began to stammer. 'Would you have some coffee, Herr Martin – a cake?'

'How nice of you to ask.' I moved towards the sitting-room door.

'Not there, Herr Martin.' Frau Glick seemed ever closer to breakdown. 'The kitchen,' she squeaked. 'More homely, more *gemütlich*.'

I was aware that Glick himself had begun another series of wild contortions which seemed to stop his wife in her tracks. They looked at each other and then shrugged. Frau Glick opened the sitting-room door and with a loud sigh beckoned me to enter.

And I could see it instantly, the reason for their pathetic embarrassment. As I looked round the room, it seemed as though it contained more of my possessions than theirs. Every book or ornament, every rug and picture and pot had been looted blind from my flat, probably the moment after I'd shut the door. I was so dumbstruck that for a few minutes I couldn't move or say a word.

'Herr Martin . . .' I could feel Glick patting my shoulder. 'Please sit down. We thought you were never coming back. They said you had gone. They said you were a traitor.'

I sat on the sofa, and the two boys came in and they all stood in front of me in a semi-circle, as though waiting for punishment. And I couldn't help feeling sorry for them with their shabby little ways, standing in their shabby little flat, with their country crumbling around them – and nothing, but nothing to be proud of in the whole, wide world.

'It's all right,' I told them. 'It's OK, I'm not coming back. Just today, really. That's all. Just today.'

They brightened up after that and Frau Glick made the best coffee I'd ever drunk out of my own cups and served a terrific apple slice, and we started to chat about the new ways – what would it mean to Germany – and we got through a lot of adjectives like 'amazing' and 'historic' and that lovely, untranslatable word *'unvoraussehbar'*, which means that you couldn't see it coming.

Pretty appropriate, when you consider how the afternoon ended.

I finished my apple slice and Glick looks at me, his face all sad and silly again, and then he asks me to follow him upstairs.

Past my old front door we go and into the corridor that led to Dortmunder's tiny hovel. Suddenly Glick stops beside the cleaner's cupboard where the brooms and mops and bins were kept, steps over them to a stack of shelves, presses a button and slides the entire wall away.

'For God's sake,' I hear myself mutter. But he doesn't say anything, simply steps forward, turns on a light, and reveals a windowless room about ten foot square, with tables and banks of tape recorders in neat rows.

I knew exactly what it was, because I had set up some of those rooms myself, but I'd had no idea they'd done it to me, right next to my flat.

'For God's sake,' I repeat. 'Who the hell did . . . ?'

'We all did,' Glick says quietly. 'One of our jobs was to monitor your conversations.'

I must have looked at him with an expression of complete incredulity.

'But in the last few years we did it only on an occasional basis,' he adds reassuringly.

'Oh good,' I reply, amazed at how easily I can still accept such a gross intrusion into my life.

'Would you like to see your own flat again?' he asks.

'No.'

But he takes me anyway, opening the door with a clutch of keys, as if he's the jailer – which I now suppose he was.

And thankfully, it wasn't really my flat at all – not any more, with the rugs torn up and the furniture taken. Just a shell of the place in which I might have had to end my days.

'Herr Martin?' Glick moves in front of me.

'What is it?'

'I thought we might have a short discussion.'

'I thought we were.'

Glick puts on his most formal of tones. 'I wanted to apologize, Herr Martin. I have been thinking a lot in the last few days.' He pauses a moment. 'Things I have never thought before.'

'And what have you concluded?'

'Herr Martin, you have spent some years in our country, and therefore you will understand what I am saying. This system, this . . .' he groped at the thin air, 'this way of life, was not what I wanted. I supported it, and defended with it, but it was not what I wanted.' He leans against the wall as if needing support. 'I come from Dresden, Herr

Martin. I came here in 'sixty-four. I saw the Wall, not once, not twice, but a thousand times. Everywhere I went it stood in front of my nose. I became obsessed with it. I started dreaming of what it was like on the other side, the lights, the people in bright clothes . . .'

'What happened?'

'The dream went away.' He shakes his head. 'But not the anger. You see, Herr Martin, the system was just. Not all of it, but the centre, the essence. And yet I could never tolerate the stupidity of those in power . . . the daily doses of nonsense from the Central Committee, from the newspapers, how everything was wonderful, and beautiful and we were the happiest in the world. Intellectually, it was nothing short of criminal. I still feel that way.'

'You could have done something about it.'

Glick winced, as if I'd hit a nerve. 'Perhaps, Herr Martin, this is the greatest tragedy of all. We ourselves should have done something to change it. We should have stood up and protested. We should have rattled the gates . . .' He stopped for a moment to catch his breath. 'We did not have the courage, Herr Martin, and for that we have paid the price, and will pay it for years to come.'

I look around the bare hallway, but there's nothing to sit on. 'Was there anything good about it?'

Glick smiles sadly. 'How can you ask such a

question, Herr Martin? We had theatre and con-
certs and cheap museums, we would talk of
philosophy and love and friendship – but that too
will be swept away. The Wall hasn't just come
down. They won and we lost. They are *"Die
Sieger"* – the victors. You know there was another
dream that some of us had, and that was of opening
the Wall and creating a country which had the best
of the East and the best from the West.' He laughs a
dry, brittle laugh. 'It can't happen. We lost, and
they won and in a few months everything that we
had will be down the drain. We won't be talking
about things that matter, it will be *"Geld"* – money.
Money this, money that and the envy that goes with
it. You will see, Herr Martin.' He shakes a finger at
me. 'You will see.'

For the first time I have nothing to say to him.

'I'll leave you here by yourself for a moment,'
says Glick with mock solemnity. 'I'll be downstairs.'

Which gives me the opportunity to get out of the
place again without seeing him. I take a quick look
out of the kitchen window and that hasn't changed,
and then tread the bare boards towards the corridor, down the stone steps and away into the street.
And I could imagine the Glicks sitting round their
tea table – my tea table – wondering where I was,
and then as the minutes tick by, realizing with total
incomprehension that I had had to get out of there,
and couldn't bear to see them again.

By this time, though, my mind is on other things. I look at my watch. Only two or three hours left before the rendezvous. And then, maybe, I'd know the last and most important of all the facts.

And then again, maybe you won't, says the black dog, who's begun trotting with me down the street, as if we're old friends.

# THIRTY-EIGHT

So why didn't I see it coming? I still don't know.

I was back at Christian's house two hours before the scheduled departure. But they were tense, as they always were, and there was beer and whisky on the table, and there shouldn't have been either.

Schmidt was upstairs in his room, Keen in the kitchen, Niki and Christian checking their weapons.

'Where's Clarky?'

'Last-minute stuff,' said Christian. 'He'll meet us there.'

I sat in the living room, newly cleansed and sanitized, the ashtrays emptied, the tins and packets of food assembled and thrown away. We'd had our time there. We were moving out.

But it wasn't right. I kept remembering the words they'd always thrown at us in the Service, 'You get out of an operation what you put in', and this time we were understaffed and under-supported like never before.

You see – even when a single agent went over the

Wall, the back-up was enormous. Teams of radio monitors would scour the police and security networks for hours, other teams would check out the location before, maybe the Americans would be alerted. Each agent was worth the full resources that the Service had to offer. And he went over knowing he had them.

That night, truth to tell, we had nothing.

Shortly before ten, Keen called me in to the study.

'You know what to do?' he asked.

'Of course not.'

Keen sighed. 'Clarky has fixed it. You're just there to babysit. You hand over Schmidt and they'll give you a file, or a name, or an event.'

'They could tell us anything.'

'They won't. Look Martin. The Russians ordered the Wall to come down – and so it did. It was a symbol. They told this to the West Germans. The old bets are off. The old operations are over.'

'So they're just lining up like good little boys, ready to own up.'

'I didn't say that. They've decided for whatever reason – I suspect it was West German money – to close the door on the East. They're getting out, taking what they want, leaving the rest, and trying as hard as ever to penetrate the new order.' He pointed a finger at me. 'Only maybe some of their own agents don't like the new order. Maybe some of them can't be trusted any more. Maybe the ones who worked in the old system should be pensioned off before they become unreliable. If we're worried about our people, they're just as worried about theirs.'

'Why don't they simply turn up, kill us and get it over with?'

'They want us to believe it's over and take that message home. They want some credibility, even some trust. And besides I'll be there too. They don't murder intelligence chiefs.'

'Why not?'

'Against the rules.'

We left the house in two cars. Schmidt with Niki and Christian in the first. Keen and I following behind, the traffic sparse, the rain blurring our view through the windscreen.

Clarky had said 'Steinstücken' which wasn't just an odd place for a rendezvous, it was one of the strangest locations in all of Berlin. A tiny Western enclave of a dozen houses, stuck at the end of a long tube-like access road in the middle of the East German countryside. When they drew up the demarcation lines at the end of the war, someone must have forgotten about this place and then, only as an afterthought, built a tiny road with a wall on either side, to let the residents in and out.

We were to wait for ten minutes. If no one showed, we should head home and try again the next day.

On our instructions Christian had switched on a transmitter in his car, and so we could hear Schmidt, foul-mouthed and offensive, straining at the handcuffs that held him.

I'd seen the same thing with farm animals on their way to market – they became anxious and restive, sometimes they even made a break for it, sensing by means of some deep, primeval intuition that they were about to die.

After a while Christian told him to shut-the-fuck-up and in the end we, too, switched him off because he reminded us of consciences that we no longer possessed.

I know that we in the West always claimed the moral high ground when it came to our more shady dealings. But it wasn't justified. We used their methods and they used ours. You simply chose your side and got on with it.

As the lights streamed past, I shut my eyes and wondered how I'd look on this night in the years to come. Whatever the outcome I couldn't have gone on living like that, my strings pulled first by one group, then another.

The KGB had begun it, killing their way almost casually around Berlin, hounding me from the city. They'd shot the liaison officer who visited me, they murdered Frau Ansbach, they'd even had a go at me – perhaps to spur me into action.

And then it seemed to suit both sides for me to search out a traitor, whose identity had been lost.

To America, then back to Britain, and again to Berlin, where the traitor would finally show his hand or end the game.

I looked across at Keen, driving calmly and without effort, his frame housed in a black trench-coat, a blue seaman's cap on his head. He was whistling gently through his teeth – such a tiny safety valve for all the fears he had to be carrying.

Without warning I was jarred awake, as Keen hit the brakes. The car skidded slightly. We seemed to be in a wood. Through the trees I could see the clouds rushing past at about a thousand feet, the moon riding in and out of view.

Christian had pulled up about fifteen yards ahead. As I rubbed the condensation from the windscreen I could see him get out and run towards us.

Keen wound down his window.

'About half a mile further,' said Christian. 'From now on we're in the border zone. If anyone is still working over there, they'll be able to track us – sound and vision. So better say nothing.'

And now we crawled along, without even our sidelights, because even if they know you're there, you offer no free gifts and no helping hands. If they really want you, you make them work for it.

Down the guarded lane we went – and I have never in my life felt more exposed, the Wall on either side, the remains of East Germany beyond it, and an enemy who won't show himself till he's ready.

*I hope you know what you're doing, Clarky. I hope you've checked and re-checked this one, because I'm scared rigid and I don't want to go home in a box.*

There wasn't a single light in the enclave. Just clumps of trees and houses and a few cars left deserted. We stopped in the car park where the tourist buses used to bring all the gawkers and snappers from the world outside. Wish they were here now.

Christian back again beside our window.

'Five minutes to eleven,' he announced as if he's the only one with a working watch. 'What now?'

'Leave Schmidt in the car,' said Keen. 'Get over to the houses, watch from there. C'mon!' He beckoned for me to follow, and we didn't hang around because now the sky had cleared and the moon was almost on top of us.

We squatted down beside a low wall, the car some fifty yards away, and Christian had a machine pistol in his hand, and a coatful of other arms that he pushed in our direction.

'Help yourself, Herr Martin,' he said with undue politeness. 'A matter of confidence, *Ja*? Nothing more.'

I delved in and brought out a small Italian automatic, Keen chose a revolver. And I'm thinking . . . I'm out of my depth here. If anyone starts shooting I'm the last one to shoot back. We're outgunned, and outmanoeuvred and we haven't even seen the enemy.

Something less than dangerous, we sat there, trying to track the noises of the night. And then Christian was on his feet, cursing like mad and our eyes turn instinctively to the car. Even at this distance we can see the movement, and hear the engine, and then we were out there running like hell because it looked as though the worst thing in the world was happening . . .

Schmidt seemed to have lunged at Niki, hit him in the face, caught him off guard – something like that. For the shape of Niki was slumped against his door and the car was moving, with Schmidt leaning over the lifeless shape, trying to get his feet to the pedals.

Christian was there first, grabbing the door handle, but it's locked, he can't get a grip and the car is spinning on the gravel, as Schmidt kicks his foot on to the accelerator.

I recall now, seeing Christian thrown clear, recall the dust and the shouts and the moon looking down coldly as if nothing were going on – the car gathering speed – and then my mind seems to play tricks on me.

Was there a light at the end of the access road? Some shapes? The three of us were standing in the car park, and we all heard it – the sudden crack of glass and metal, but we couldn't see anything until way down the road, the brake lights of the car came on and seemed to dance around in a strange circle.

We were running again, with Keen shouting something I couldn't hear – and then we didn't need to run any more. For just ahead of us, you could see the car, slewed over on its side, the front slammed into the Wall, and there were all too many of those shapes, that I might or might not have seen before.

There must have been ten or twelve of them, in black fatigues, with weapons they knew how to use. And they'd simply scaled the Wall from East to West, because there were some ropes hanging loosely, all the way to the ground.

For the moment they weren't interested in us. Two of them were forcing open the car door, dragging Schmidt out by his handcuffs. And isn't it strange how the most shocking events, often appear the most random and casual? For quite by chance it seemed, one of them bent down over the struggling, moaning figure, pressed a long, silenced barrel against his head and fired. And with equal nonchalance, the body of Schmidt, just seemed to give up and slump to the ground, with all the life-force punctured out of it, its business completed, its cycle run, that night on a tiny road in Berlin.

They formed a wide circle around us, and I only remember wondering what was taking them so long, and being shocked most of all by the sound of a helicopter that seemed to swoop at us from over the Wall, like an animal in panic, reminding me that the world had once again turned on its head – and that death and violence ruled, as they always had done, supreme.

## THIRTY-NINE

They knew who they wanted. Christian was left behind, so was Niki. And I can still recall them standing on that road, cowed and frightened in the moonlight, as Keen and I were bent double beneath the rotor blades of the helicopter and pushed inside.

We took off straight into the wind, but we didn't climb. The pilot flew fast and low, and it seemed that if I'd leaned out I could have touched the fields and the trees that passed beneath us. I guessed we were heading East. Just forty miles to the Polish border, only we wouldn't be stopping there.

In the distance, lay towns and cities, marked out by the cheap blue streetlamps and the yellow lights on the cars, but we veered away from them, the helicopter leaning and clawing at the night air.

Two guards sat either side of us – young, hard profiles, moulded only for the violence they'd shown. As the miles fell away no one moved or spoke, our thoughts crushed out of us by the beating of the rotors.

Keen shut his eyes, and maybe he was reviewing

his precious theories, or working out how to save his neck. But he gave no sign. There were moments when I could have torn him apart and others when I wanted to lean over and touch his arm, and tell him that at least we'd tried, and it wasn't such a tragedy to try and then lose.

But there is nothing, I've discovered, that sits so heavily as a failed theory – especially when your life depends on it.

An hour was to pass before we landed and refuelled. Through the perspex window I could make out a narrow runway, with a truck and an unmarked Niva jeep – and I didn't like the look of that, still less the look of the driver and the Soviet army flashes on his uniform. And now there could be no doubt at all about the direction we were headed.

Why had it gone so wrong? Why had the rendezvous been blown? Clarky, I thought, what black hole can have swallowed you, which step did you miss, who stabbed you when you were so close to home?

I must have dozed for a while, for I remember Keen pulling at my shoulder and being surprised that the guards didn't prevent him.

'Martin,' he kept repeating, 'Martin don't give up for God's sake. Stay strong.'

And for some reason I laughed, although I don't think he heard me above the noise of the engines. Here was this pathetic old man, too blind to see that his number had been called, clinging to some strange, misguided faith, out of his time. Keen the wise and supercilious, Keen the thinker and the knower, the plotter and planner – all gone to hell in a helicopter.

I pushed his hand away, because if this were all going to end, I wanted my last thoughts to be my own, not Keen's. It had become bitterly cold and my head ached violently, and I wanted to go anywhere but Russia.

Abruptly one of the guards reached for his headset and listened. Then he clapped his colleague's shoulder and gave a thumbs-up sign and I guessed that meant we had crossed the border.

I looked through the window and tried to remember the last time. That memorable little trip some four years before, when the Stasi had sent me to Moscow for de-briefing.

By then, of course, I was trusted, I was established. The quicksand was holding.

'No cause for alarm, Herr Martin,' Kirsch had said at the time, with an expression that indicated there was probably every cause. 'They wish to ask some questions and check some answers. A get-to-know-you session. *Ja*?'

The man who met me at Moscow airport was affable and amusing, fresh from his posting in London, a rounded jovial little fat-boy, a raconteur and a linguist, the proud possessor, he declared, of the largest collection of anti-government jokes in the Soviet Union. He was also a colonel in the KGB.

I was aching from laughter by the time I reached the Lubyanka on Dzherzhinksy Square – and how many people have ever said that?

Within an hour of arriving I had a glass of pepper vodka in my hand, a sliver of black bread straining under a dollop of caviar, and an open-sounding invitation to, 'Look over the place and meet people.'

It turned out to be a trip around Moscow having lunch. A chief of Directorate one day, a policy co-ordinator the next, a couple of European experts. *Blinis* and more caviar. Back to the office – and an endless monologue from a pair of haggard old crows who'd apparently toured Europe in the sixties, tempting Nato diplomats into sordid indiscretions. One could only wonder how.

At any rate, by the final evening, I was bewildered and disoriented, and no wiser about the purpose of my trip.

True, they had asked questions. But if they hadn't known the answers already they should have been taken out into the backyard and forcibly separated from their genitals. Toy questions like, Who was in which department back in London? What was the relationship with the Foreign Office? How much did the Prime Minister really get told?

For their part they had given away less than a second-hand guidebook. A few impressions, a few faces and a lot of harmless in house gossip. I went to bed in my hundred-dollar-a-night room at the National Hotel, with the unerring sensation that I was missing something.

It wasn't till three o'clock that morning that I found out what it was.

I didn't just hear a knock at the door. What I really heard was the sound of a fire axe splintering it down the middle. I was aware of at least two pairs of hands lifting, and slamming me into the wall, and then a rapid and unnatural movement through the air until I landed on the floor and lost consciousness.

I returned to the world in a waiting room. At least it looked like that. A dull, grey rectangle with cheap plastic chairs along each wall, a low table in the middle with odd newspapers and dirty ashtrays. Every so often the place seemed to shake and I became aware of the intermittent clatter of trains.

My fat little friend from the KGB sat by the window, reading from a sheaf of papers. He looked up, but the amiable smile and the friendly demeanour had gone.

'You're going home,' he said, and it was a quiet, non-committal statement.

'I was going home anyway . . .'

'And so you were,' he replied, 'only this is a land of great contrasts my friend, and it was only fair you should see some of them before you leave.

Familiarization, I think you call it. You wouldn't want to take home the message that all we do in Moscow is have lunch. Would you?'

He had mastered all the idioms. He'd bathed in the language, and drunk it and embraced its cadences. And yet he'd brought to it his Slavic fervour and passion. English but not English. Never English, because he'd only ever do it one way, for one truth, for one master. He could never think himself into all the thousand prejudices, and complexes and distinctions that mark out the English. To be blunt, he had no class – of *any* kind. He would never know the value of an understatement, nor the limits of excess. He might win at chess, but he'd lose the egg-and-spoon race. The sublime and the ridiculous would for ever pass him by – that combination which separates the English from the rest of the world.

I looked at him and smiled. 'Whatever you say, comrade.'

He got up and beckoned me to the door. I swayed a little and a sharp pain cut across my forehead, but I followed.

Down to a platform, cold and grey and provincial, filled with the masses. I realized suddenly I had no possessions and no money.

'Thirty-six hours to Berlin,' he said and handed me a ticket. 'I regret it was not possible to book a seat. So many people travelling at this time of year.' The smile returned.

'You shouldn't have bothered,' I told him. 'It would have been nicer to walk.'

'My friend, I hope sincerely that you remember your time here. We have the impression the Stasi often plays games with us. You forget that a few years ago we forced the Germans back *before* Moscow. These days it is we who pick the battle-fields.' He turned to go, but then looked back again. 'Treat us right, and we will do the same. Play games, and we will play them better. Have a pleasant journey.'

Of course, looking back, it was the most unpleasant journey I could possibly have had – unless you count the helicopter that was now returning me, by all indications, to the same place.

I wouldn't have minded so much, but it appeared we were coming to land. Another unmarked runway glided into view, only this one was well lit up with soldiers ringing the perimeter. And the face so clearly visible among them was that of my fat little colonel in the KGB, substantially fatter than he had been, but altogether unforgettable.

Hard to escape is the memory of Clarky standing next to him, apparently laughing his head off.

# FORTY

A lot of people these days seem pretty unconcerned about treachery. I'm not.

All right, times have changed, the battles are different. Friends and enemies have been jumbled around. But the principle is the same. People like me were paid to keep some secrets untold and find others out. And if it's too grand and woolly to speak of the national interest – then think of it simply as a job, and you do it the way the client wants.

So when I saw Clarky, standing fat and sassy on a runway in the Soviet Union, it wasn't just the feeling that he'd cocked his leg on all of us, but that it was unprofessional and unworthy. Clarky, like the other half of the human race, was therefore also a shit, deserving of our contempt.

We didn't greet each other. Keen, shaking either from cold or rage, was unable to speak. The fat-boy smiled unpleasantly, barely able to contain his excitement, but Clarky was businesslike and in a hurry, leading me to a hangar.

I was glad to see his back still caused him pain.

He stood crooked and awkward and looked over my shoulder towards the others, as if worried that they would hear what he said.

'We don't have long, Martin.'

'Everyone tells me that.'

'Think what you like,' he said. 'But I made a deal for you. Not quite the one you thought. But at least you'll find out what you wanted.'

'I just have. I don't want to discuss it any further.' And I really didn't, standing, freezing on a Soviet airfield, hating most of mankind, and Clarky in particular.

'All right.' He lifted both palms, as if to restrain me. 'Just listen.' He put a hand on his spine and grimaced at the discomfort. 'A lot of people over here don't think I should be talking to you at all, and a lot of people would prevent it if they knew. So this is going to be quick, and then you're getting out of here.'

'You're too generous,' I said.

He wiped his forehead with a handkerchief. Despite the cold he seemed to be sweating heavily.

'I began working for the Soviets, just before I was thrown out of the Service. I'd gone back to cocaine despite all the treatment, and instead of using that against me, they helped me give it up, actually helped pay for the treatment.'

'The Russians are wonderful,' I replied. 'You should have seen the kindly way they treated Schmidt.'

'Schmidt was a killer. One of the high-ups in the Stasi. You know that. It was settling a score. He'd done the same. Anyway,' he looked hurriedly at his watch, 'I didn't do it for the help they gave me. I was thinking about the future . . .'

'Don't make me laugh.'

'Not mine. But the way things were going – in general. The changes in Europe. The need to democratize, to speed things up. Only the Russians were doing it. I gave Moscow the names of our agents in East Germany. They asked me for them. I handed them over. They in turn passed them to the Stasi.'

'You could face a death sentence for that.'

He shook his head. 'It wouldn't come to court, Martin – not this one.'

'And why is that?'

'Just listen to what I say. Things were changing in Russia, but not in East Germany. Tension was growing between them, and Moscow made the decision to help get rid of the leadership in Berlin.'

'So why . . . ?'

He ignored me. 'But to do that, they had to get closer to them, get inside the Stasi headquarters, create some trust, really make them believe they were still on the same side.'

'So that's why you gave them the names of our agents.'

'Right.'

'You really are a perverted kind of shit.'

'There was no other way. Once the names were handed over, relations warmed up. We,' he shook his head. 'Moscow got the access it wanted, the co-operation, and we could slip people in under their noses, with no questions asked. When the time came, we could pull all the strings we needed from the inside and topple the leadership . . .'

'And then I arrived . . .'

'And then you arrived,' he repeated. 'And the pressure was on. To be frank, after that East German visited you, offering information, Moscow wanted you dead, along with everyone else. That's why the little nun was dispatched from Berlin to do the deed. Only when she failed some people began to think again. Maybe you didn't know very much after all, but more importantly maybe you could carry a message.'

'About an old operation?'

Clarky grinned. 'So you worked that bit out . . .'

'It wasn't difficult, considering where Fenton and that Soviet diplomat were murdered.'

'That was the reason they lifted me.' Clarky looked around him. 'The Stasi were still too good, too dangerous. You know, we were going to deal with Fenton — for the same reason I'm dealing with you. For the same reason you were brought here. We were going to give him my name, come clean about the carve-up operation between the superpowers. No more dividing the world into spheres of influence or economic zones. But most important, we had to make sure everyone realized it was over. Moscow was insistent about that. They wanted the file closed.'

'Why?'

'You know why. The Soviet Union is in economic crisis, there's hunger, the shortages are worse than ever. The Kremlin badly needs some goodwill – and this is one way they can get it. They need credibility. They need cash – now.'

'So they orchestrated everything for me to carry back that message?'

'Right. They even blew up my house, thinking you couldn't possibly suspect me after that. They saw to it that you were protected in America. They even believed for a while they could disguise my identity and leave me where I was.'

'You're all mad.'

'Unfortunately there's a group in the Kremlin that agrees with you. They thought we were playing games. Much better to get rid of you as planned, and then in all likelihood me as well . . .'

Abruptly Clarky broke off. Without warning there was the deadening noise of a plane flying low overhead. We both ducked instinctively. Fat-boy ran over and grabbed Clarky's arm.

'Not good news, my friend. It's a military plane. Someone seems to have found out where we are . . .'

Clarky began moving towards the hangar door.

'Where the hell are we?' I shouted.

'Ukraine,' he yelled back. 'Just over the Polish border.'

'Christ almighty!'

We were out now on the tiny airfield, running in the dawn light for the helicopter, the soldiers still surrounding it, uncertain what to do.

The fat-boy shouted something at them, and they began dispersing, the rifles coming down from their shoulders. In the distance I could see the transport plane, tree-hopping, coming in for final approach.

Inside the helicopter the pilot must have switched on the engines because the rotor blade began turning with almost pathetic slowness. Keen was being shoved into the cockpit. I turned to Clarky.

'I wasn't the only one who protected you,' he said and smiled for the first time. 'You had all sorts of friends looking after you.'

The noise of the helicopter was louder, much louder. Right at the end of the runway, I saw the wheels of the transport plane hit the ground.

Fat-boy was grabbing Clarky's arm. From the cockpit window the pilot was beckoning me violently.

'Don't forget.' And now I don't remember if I heard him or whether, by this time, I was reading his lips. 'I wasn't alone in this. Couldn't have done it by myself. You have to know that.' Clarky shouting into the wind.

I grabbed the side of the helicopter. The noise was searing. Someone was pulling me inside and the great machine was lifting, and I could see Clarky and the fat-boy running for the perimeter. And there on the runway, the transport plane was disgorging the first of its troops, only from high above they looked like dozens of insects fanning out across the countryside. You didn't need to be long-sighted to see the weapons in their hands, didn't need extra-sensory hearing to catch the small-arms fire, and the thud of something much larger.

And then? And then nothing – cloud over Poland, as if we'd gone into another world. No Russia, suddenly, no Clarky, we were heading fast towards Berlin, with Keen sitting almost motionless, his head in his hands and his feet drumming on the cockpit floor.

I never heard what happened to Clarky and the fat-boy and I never cared enough to find out.

Maybe he wasn't as lousy as I'd first thought. Maybe he was. Time often blurs your judgement. In any case, as I said before, some people are pretty unconcerned these days about treachery. But I'm not one of them.

## FORTY-ONE

The helicopter dipped down into Steinstücken and took off again the moment we touched the ground. I would have waved to the pilot, thanked him maybe, but he didn't even look round. God alone knew who he answered to or where he was going.

Keen was exhausted. His face had turned the kind of mottled grey that old people acquire when they've gone too far. I dragged him half asleep into the hotel and left him on his bed.

And now I'm in my room, tired as a dog, but I keep playing back the words Clarky shouted into the sky. 'I wasn't alone, couldn't have done it by myself.' And suddenly I don't want to know what he meant. I've had enough answers, because these days all the answers seem to mean bodies, and it is surely time the dying ceased.

While I slept they put a note under my door. Iris's note, but I didn't find it till midday.

'And by the time you get this,' she had written, 'I will be well away from here.'

Perhaps 'note' is the wrong word. It was more of a little book than anything else. A detail-by-detail account of the times she had spent with Clarky, leaving in all the impressions, the throwaway lines, the gestures. Quite enough for me to put the story together.

Twenty pages in all, and she had written at the end, 'I don't agree with what he's done. That's why I've put all this down. You probably want to know if I love him. Well, maybe I do and maybe I don't. But he's the only landmark I have. The rest is just streets and towns and days and nights and people that I'll never really get to know. But I know Clarky and I'll be all right with him.'

I showed it to Keen when he woke up, and he put it rudely in his pocket and said he'd read it later, when the 'whole thing' was wrapped up.

And I couldn't help thinking it was sad she would get all the way to Moscow, and no one would tell her what had happened to Clarky. And maybe after days or weeks, of waiting in corridors and telephoning and getting nowhere, as only happens in Russia, she would be shown a death certificate, or told to write a letter to a prison, or sent home with nothing at all. And Iris seemed to deserve better than that.

We went out into the streets and Keen hailed a cab, and said 'Checkpoint Charlie,' to the driver, and turned to me and muttered, 'While it's still there.'

He didn't talk along the way. When we got there, he climbed out and started walking towards the barrier. I paid the taxi and caught up with him.

'You're not going over, are you?'

'Time I had a glance at it.' He was his old, gruff, distant self. 'Don't worry,' he said. 'I made a phone call this morning, cleared it with all the elders and betters.'

It was a perfunctory look at the passports, because the border wasn't going to be there for long. Where before it had appeared vibrant and deadly, it now seemed like one of those ancient torture devices, grimy and stained and cruelly pointless. There was a smell of old evil in the place, that was to persist long after the horror and the politics that created it, had moved on.

Keen looked down the Friedrichstrasse towards Unter Den Linden and sighed, as if he'd just settled a private bet.

'We'll talk now,' he said. 'And then we won't talk again, all right? Seems appropriate that we get things out of the way here. Mm?'

And here even the green trees looked grey. Beside them, though, tiny markets were waking up. Shop windows were covered in stickers proclaiming the jewels of the new era – holidays in Italy, bananas, hotdogs from the West. Cars that drove.

'You know,' said Keen, 'or maybe you don't. But if you'd stayed over here in your basket, none of this would have happened.'

'I didn't really *have* a basket any more, if you remember.'

He nodded. 'But when you surfaced everyone had to start looking for the real traitor. In our own way we'd buried it, removed most of the people involved, blamed it on you, written it off as a normal business loss. But then the East Germans wanted to find that traitor too.'

'Why? What was so important about it for them?'

'Schmidt thought he could use it against the West. If he could find the man's identity, then he could get all the facts about the deal between Moscow and Washington. I suspect what he wanted to do was to threaten both capitals that he'd go public with the story, unless they made him a decent offer.'

'But the deal was off . . .'

'Yes. By then it was. Trouble with Glasnost was that once they'd got it on the road, things started to come out. In the end they thought it was far too risky.'

'So Clarky could have lived out his days in Oxford and nothing would have happened to him . . .'

'That's about it.' Keen sat down on a park bench. More trees, a damp plot of untended grass. Some potted humanity. I recalled what a colleague in the Service had once said about East German policy, 'Give them a tree to look at and a sausage to eat, and bugger the rest.' And when you looked around, they pretty well had.

So now we're there, I thought. Keen had said

we'd talk about it just once and never again, and the time had come.

'Clarky's final words,' I said and looked at Keen, hoping he'd finish the sentence.

'Oh yes. Well that's it, isn't it? The other part of the deal. Who else had an interest in helping Moscow penetrate the Stasi? Who else wanted to see the East German leadership toppled, and the new order go through?'

We were silent for a few moments. Then Keen stood up and began walking again.

'This is where it gets into theory,' he said quietly. 'We'll never know and they'll never tell us. But let me try to sketch the picture.' He looked round as if to make sure I was listening. 'The Americans were getting increasingly pissed off with the Europeans. Trade mainly. They didn't like the way the EC was talking unity and they were getting left in the cold. You have to remember they think globally, and when you do that, the rest of the world's your backyard and when anything happens anywhere, you're involved.'

'Except they weren't.'

'That's what they disliked. So when there was a chance of carving things up with the Russians, they took it. And if they could smooth a little democracy in along the way, then so much the better . . .'

'Are you saying they turned a blind eye when our networks were blown?'

'I'm saying they did nothing to help. I'm saying

the Russians cleared it with them. Who knows they may even have provided some names. Clarky didn't know all of them – which is why we never really thought it was him.'

'Do you think Cassie knew about this?'

Keen walked on for a while and didn't say anything and I went and stood in front of him and repeated the question.

'You know what I say,' he looked hard at me, then turned away. 'I say we leave it there. I say we just close the book, and throw it on the rest of the pile and burn the lot. I say there's no point now in going further.'

And he wouldn't talk any more. In an uncanny way he led me back towards the checkpoint, as if, somehow he'd known the way round East Berlin all his life. We passed just as smoothly through passport control – and now I could see why Keen had gone over when he had, and why his own time was running out. There it stood, the black car with the British number plates, parked by the Allied Checkpoint, the guardians, getting out and standing there, those men in grey suits, those unseen, unnamed servants of our crown.

Keen grinned sheepishly. 'You see, they don't think they know me any more,' he said quietly. 'Even me. Am I an old man who's gone round the bend, or a trustworthy servant of Her Majesty? Have we just been strolling in East Berlin, or plotting the downfall of the Western world?' He giggled. 'They don't know,' he added. 'Just don't know.'

I walked with him, towards the car and I wasn't going to ask but I couldn't help it. 'What am I supposed to do now?'

'The decent thing, Martin, the decent thing.' Keen didn't look at me and his voice had dropped to a whisper, so that I could pretend to myself at such future time as I might need to, that he hadn't really spoken at all.

Americans call it plausible deniability. And that's the age we live in.

## FORTY-TWO

And now?

You can see it, can't you?

Martin going to Washington, pushing his feet in front of him, up the path on Brandywine Street, knocking and trembling a little at the great house door.

It was the kind of November morning that the city excels at. The wind was gentle, the sun warm, as if autumn were not long past and spring not far away.

Cassie came out on to the porch shielding her eyes from the light. 'I haven't been out much,' she told me, and led me back inside where she'd been sorting through her life, she said, to see what was left.

I didn't stay long that day. She was tired and fragile and it never occurred to me to ask her questions.

I came the next day and the day after, and by the end of the week she was returning to me – in smiles and the touch of her hands and in the light that came from her eyes, and the kindness and warmth behind them.

So I stayed that week and the next – and somehow she never asked me if I were leaving again, and I never suggested it.

In time we sold the big house and moved into the city. It's a terraced house in Georgetown, that she fills with toys and pictures and friends and all the things and people that make her happy. We often eat out, the way we once said we would, and we travel and for me, the world is back in its orbit. I have a home.

Seldom do I think of the years I lost in the East bloc. There's now a generation that doesn't even know where it was or what it meant. Someone even asked me whether East Germany had been a country. And I couldn't answer, because it wasn't a proper one – and if people are really beginning to forget its existence, then that can only be good. It deserves no eulogies.

We once took a trip back to England so I could visit my mother's grave. Perhaps I wanted to tell her it was over, tell her what really happened, try to explain why she had to die in so much disappointment.

For a long time I stood by her headstone, listening to the wind talking through the trees. After half an hour an old priest came bounding up the path, chattering about Cyril and Betty and Lynn, as if I'd known them or should have done. And I had no idea if they were among the cemetery's permanent inmates or still walking around in fine health.

At any rate he wished me good luck and, at that point, the sun dived back behind the clouds and the rain came in torrents.

He fled, and I stayed where I was, saying 'goodbye' and 'sorry' to my mother and not having sufficient faith to believe she could hear me.

But I'm back now in America. Cassie has returned to her old subject – communications, which she teaches part-time at Georgetown University and I'm a consultant to a firm of lawyers, drumming up new business in the Eastern part of Europe. I told them it was like chucking money into a black hole, but they said I shouldn't pass that on to the clients.

In fact they don't know quite as much about me as they think they do. The Service was kind enough to give me references for jobs I'd never done in places I'd seldom if ever visited. And otherwise they have kept away from me, knowing I wouldn't ever re-open the issue, and knowing the reason why.

You see, not even Cassie and I have ever talked about Berlin. I want her to be free of the past, not weighted down by it. Even now there are times when she seems to walk paths where I can't follow, when she recalls events and actions that I know nothing about.

But then – and I've never said this before – I have a secret place of my own.

It's a place where the questions seem to come at

315

me from shadows, where I hear the voices of Kirsch or Schmidt or Frau Ansbach, but can make no sense of what they're saying. Questions about whether Cassie knew what was happening to me, whether she could have helped me, whether she even allowed all those agents to be betrayed.

Cassie, I sometimes say your name to myself and wonder about such things. And often you look at me as if you know full well what I'm doing, just as you know that I can never ever bring myself to ask you those questions out loud.

This, though, is yours – if you should wish to read it.

# THE SPY IN QUESTION
by Tim Sebastian

Dmitry Kalyagin's cover is unravelling. For twenty
years he's been a mole inside the Soviet Union's
Politburo, where the opportunities for espionage are
unprecedented, but so are the dangers of discovery.
Now the KGB is pursuing him . . . the woman who
recruited him is on a personal vendetta . . . British
Intelligence is pressing for more information . . . and
Kalyagin has only two choices left: when and how to
die.

'Fast-paced, exciting reading, set in the real Moscow
of grime and icy grit'
*Washington Post*

'A pulsating thriller . . . A great read. An authentic
feel'
*Irish Press*

A Bantam Paperback

0 553 17524 6

# SPY SHADOW
by Tim Sebastian

In the snows of Southern Poland an underground leader is found dead. In Warsaw a priest betrays his calling. In London's King's Cross an old man with a dangerously long memory is murdered.

British agent James Tristram believes they are all part of the same puzzle, a puzzle whose missing pieces can only be found in Poland.

But he has unseen enemies in both Moscow and London. Two men want Tristram dead, and between them they have the power to provoke a bloody uprising that could rock the Communist world.

As time runs out, Tristram must confront them in a final act of betrayal in a lonely Polish village the world will never forget – Auschwitz.

'Crisp and taut'
*The Times*

'Set to rival John Le Carré . . . this is a political thriller with real immediacy: meaty and gripping, a frightening book, full of atmosphere'
*Good Housekeeping*

A Bantam Paperback

0 553 40055 X

## SAVIOUR'S GATE
by Tim Sebastian

Each night a small jet leaves Moscow heading for a lonely outpost in the frozen Soviet North. It takes no passengers and brings none back.

Intelligence shows this is neither a cargo flight nor a military flight. The British believe it's an escape route for the beleaguered General Secretary, who will use it, just moments before he's toppled from power.

But to do so he must first pass through the deadly Saviour's Gate in the Kremlin itself. And if he makes it that far, who can he turn to? Who has to die to save him?

'Probably the best novel since *The Spy Who Came In From The Cold*'
*Stephen Coonts*

'Absorbing, tense, and all too credible . . . this is all a prophetic thriller should be'
*Observer*

'Lucid, intelligent and utterly absorbing'
*Daily Mail*

A Bantam Paperback

0 553 40056 8